THE FOOL'S PATH

ARCANA

Charity's Story

THE FOOL'S PATH

THE MAGUS'S HOUSE

THE HIGH PRIESTESS'S VIGIL

THE FOOL'S PATH

To Terry – because you are awesome..

H. T. Brady

Published by H. T. Brady
www.arcananovels.com
ISBN: 978-1-7324001-0-8
First Edition: May 2018

Cover Illustration and Design by
Kaija Saaremäel and Silver Saaremäel

For Damian.
Always

Prologue

YOU KNOW TAROT DECKS, RIGHT? Fortunetelling cards with pretty art, usually wielded by someone wearing a lot of scarves. Some of the cards have names that sound close to standard playing cards: The Ten of Wands. The Queen of Swords. Twos and Fours and Aces. Some have more dramatic names: The Fool or the Star. Death. The more normal sounding ones are the Minor Arcana, the numbered cards and their courts. The special sounding ones are the Major Arcana.

All of them are powerful magical bastards.

The tarot are alive and, sideways of this world, there's a City where they rule through magic and intrigue—and the occasional murder, if we're being honest about it. It's a dangerous place, but beautiful too. Enchanting, in all its squalor and all its glory.

Why am I telling you this?

Well, that's Delia's fault. She's the one who told me to write it all down. I've got the first parts written out—*mostly* how they happened. I'm pretty happy with it—even if it doesn't make me look particularly clever. Or good. I did try to be honest about the bad stuff. Delia will let me know whether I managed to or not. Keeping me honest is one of Delia's many jobs.

Right. Where was I? The City ruled by the Arcana.

I was born in that City. I escaped when I was sixteen, and hid in the normal world for seven years. Safe from its beauty and danger both.

It was nice while it lasted. Okay, some of it was nice. Some of it was terrible and boring. Not that-

Sorry. I'm rambling aren't I? Enough of that.

My name is Charity Waits.

This is the story of how I went back.

ONE

Office Fires

MY VOICE GETS HIGHER THE angrier I get. Not in a squeaky way, not shrill. Higher and sweeter. More saccharine. The more pissed I am, the more sugary my tone gets. At work, anyway.

It helps keep me from setting things on fire.

We all have our coping mechanisms.

"I'm terribly sorry, Mr. Saunders," I said into the phone. "I don't see..."

"Well, you should be! That order was placed two days ago and—" I held the phone away from my ear, not paying attention to the particulars as Mr. Saunders repeated for the fourth or fifth time how extremely disappointed he was with my lack of professionalism, my careless attitude, etc... etc...

I looked again through the pile of printed orders in the inbox on my desk. It wasn't there. I checked my emails again. It wasn't there—not in trash, not in spam. Nowhere. He hadn't sent the order. Not that it was going to matter.

"We'll get it sorted out right away," I interrupted him with my most sugary tone. "I know it's inconvenient, but could you resend the email? I'm sorry, but I don't see..."

"Unacceptable!" spluttered Saunders on the other end.

I rolled my eyes, sparing a glance for the slightly open door behind me. My boss's office, the lair of Mr. Bellman. He was definitely listening to my apologies and becoming determined to find out what I had done wrong, so he could make my life more miserable too.

"We will resend the email *promptly*," said Mr. Saunders on the line, to remind me of my shortcomings in the area of *promptness*. "In the meantime, I would like to speak to Mr. Bellman. Now."

"Of course," I said, scratching my throat with the high register.

I put him on hold and tapped the intercom.

"Mr. Saunders would like a word. Do you have a moment for him?"

"Yes, yes. Put him through," buzzed Bellman, eager to know what I'd done wrong. I could hear his voice through the door as well. I put the call through, and pushed myself away from my desk, stretching my arms to their fullest extent and letting my head drop. I was ready to scream at the next innocent that asked me a reasonable question. Or ready to set the phone on fire. Time for a quick break.

I got up and walked through the office. The carpet was purple once, and now was trodden into dark grey. The walls had been white and were streaked and smudged into a lighter grey. Phones rang, people spoke and hundreds of fingers tapped away at keyboards—making up the soundtrack of the American Fastener office.

I ducked onto the machine room floor to get to the loading docks. Tapping keyboards were replaced by pounding machinery and the high pitched beep of forklifts backing up. The noise hit my ears, clashing with and briefly overwhelming the fury already buzzing there. I waved to the foreman who nodded sympathetically. He was a smoker. He thought I was too, and that I didn't want to smoke with all the corporate folks. He certainly didn't want to spend time with them.

I didn't either for that matter, but that's not why I came out here.

I picked an empty loading dock and slipped out the door next to it.

Outside, snow fell. It covered the black asphalt with an inch or two of slush and turned the sky as grey as the carpet inside.

I breathed in the cold air, literally cooling off helped.

Then I trotted down a few concrete steps to where a pile of broken wooden shipping pallets were waiting to be discarded or sold or whatever. I found a seriously damaged one, kicked off a chunk of it, and checked to make sure no one was watching.

It was cold enough that I was alone.

I picked up the chunk of mangled wood and threw it hard at the brick wall of the building. While it was in the air, I raised my hand and set it on fire.

It burned up fast, all my rage from the work day expended in a quick comforting burst of orange and red. It was ash by the time it hit the wall. It burst into white and black specks and floated down with the snow. I took in another deep breath of winter air and felt better.

What? Did you think I meant 'close to setting something on fire' as a metaphor?

TWO

5:58

I GOT BACK TO MY computer to find a short email from Mr. Saunders waiting for me:

> *We expect this order to be filled PROMPTLY.*
>
> *Kevin Saunders*

It wasn't the old email forwarded. The attached file had been modified five minutes ago.

I printed out the order and put it in a stack with its fellows, muttering, "Sorry, Ms. Waits, for being an abominably rude *asshole*. I just assumed that you were the incompetent one, when actually, I'm the..."

I checked the clock on my computer. 5:58. Two minutes to go. I could do this.

"Charlene!" Mr. Bellman barked at me from his office. Or not.

My name is not Charlene. People seem to have trouble remembering Charity—which is fine, since I don't like it all that much. I didn't bother to correct him. Again.

I made my way to his office door and opened it, poking my head in.

"Yes?" I asked. My voice was closer to normal, but I could feel the sugar, waiting, preparing to cover up the rage and keep the fire at bay.

"Come in here!"

I did, closing the door.

Mr. Bellman's office was an ode to several clichés. He'd framed his business school diploma and hung it on the wall, next to a department store portrait of his family—two kids and a smiling wife. I liked his wife. She made his life miserable and was always unfailingly polite to me. His desk was cluttered with golf kitsch—a tape dispenser shaped like a golfball and a daily calendar titled 365 Golf Jokes. He read the ones he liked best to me in the mornings.

The back wall of his office was one big window, looking out on the picturesque office park: an artificially made lake and more buildings like ours stretching for as far as the eye could see in the failing light. A few big potted plants crowded on the floor by the window, all of them dead or dying.

Mr. Bellman's head was as round as the golfballs he liked so much and as bald. He wore thin glasses and sported a spotty mustache over petulant lips. He'd sweated through his generic dress shirt and his tie had— you guessed it—a pattern of red flags and golf clubs.

"I spoke to Mr. Saunders," he said.

"About that—"

"He was very displeased, you know. And a displeased customer is—"

I tried to stop him before he got rolling, but it was too late:

"Mr. Bellman, there was a misunderstanding—"

"Don't interrupt me, Charlene. That's exactly the sort of thing you need to be better with! You know, a lot of people are unemployed right now. We could have someone new in your position as quickly as..."

I tried to stop listening. I unfocused my eyes, and turned them slightly behind him, through the dirty tan slated shades and out to the snow. It was dark enough that the other buildings had mostly disappeared and now it was only the high street lamps and the snow. It was almost beautiful.

"...it's important to be grateful for what you have. Gratitude, Charlene, is the secret to everything. To a happy life. You need to be more grateful for this job. There are other people out there right now, who would be shocked to see the way you..."

I'd just purged my anger, burned it away, but apparently emotions don't work like that. I was back to a combustible state of mind already.

I worked hard not to think about singeing his eyebrows or that ridiculous calendar. It had to be 6 o'clock. It had to be time to go. I turned my eyes to one of his dead plants, concentrating on not setting it on fire.

"...every putt is important to the final score..."

The poor thing was already dead.

"...your attitude reflects on the whole company..."

The leaves were definitely not smoking. I had this under control.

"...now what do you have to say for yourself?"

I snapped my attention away from the smoldering plant and back to him, and said, with the sweetest voice I had: "Mr. Saunders could not find the original email either. He sent the order and I've taken care of it."

"Ah," said Bellman.

We stared at each other, my false smile stretched to show my teeth. I'd overdone it with the plant. It was smoking.

"Well, I guess that's okay then," said Bellman. Then he sniffed and turned around.

"What the hell?"

A small yellow flame licked up the side of the dead plant. I picked up his coffee cup and dumped the cold dregs over the flames, quenching them.

"How did...?"

"May I go, Mr. Bellman?" I asked. "It's after 6."

"What? Yes. I mean, did you see?"

I left him bending over the plant, trying to figure out where a spark could possibly have come from.

I snagged my winter coat and my bag and headed for the door, my heart already lifting.

In the parking lot, I saw that Delia had already gotten to the car. She'd scraped off the snow and started the engine, bless her. I crossed the slushy lot to freedom.

When I opened the door and slid inside, it was already warm. I sighed and closed the door harder than was polite.

"Tough day, honey?" asked Delia.

Delia calls everyone 'honey' or 'darling' or 'kitten'.

Sometimes she calls me 'chérie'. It would be annoying coming from anyone else. That right there is enough to make her special. She's got enormous brown eyes and enormous brown hair—blown out in big perfect curls. She wears big earrings, bright scarves and paints her nails with glitter. Delia is as close to a ball of sunshine and rainbows as a person gets.

She and I had been roommates since college—when we graduated with degrees and debt, Delia's aunt helped us get shitty temp jobs at American Fasteners together. For now. We had plans. Just like everyone else.

"Better now," I said, looking out at the dark and snow. "Let's go home."

"Yes, ma'am," said Delia, mock serious. She put her battered Honda in gear and began to navigate the slick parking lot.

I stared out of the window, getting my chill back.

When we reached the end of the corporate driveway, marked by an illuminated plastic sign proclaiming which office building *this* one was, I thought I saw a figure standing in the snow.

It was more an odd shadow, really, the light from the sign playing tricks—the shape appeared to turn his head to watch us, tracking our car. I turned by head to squint at it too as Delia pulled out of the driveway and onto the road. I got a chill up my spine that had nothing to do with the weather. The shadow and the sign both vanished behind us.

"How about Chinese tonight, darling? It's a greasy-noodles-and-crab-rangoon sort of night."

I laughed and said: "It's a lets-not-cook-and-make-some-poor-bastard-bring-us-warm-food-through-the-snow sort of night."

"Precisely, darling," said Delia, "Precisely!"

THREE

A Deliveryman Arrives... Eventually

DELIA AND I LIVED TOGETHER on the second floor of an old house, in an old neighborhood outside of Cleveland, Ohio. The house had been redone to fit two families and it was one of those old Tudor places from the 1920s— wooden beams and white plaster on the outside with leaded diamond patterned windows. It was drafty in the winter, but that was a great an excuse for Delia's fleece blanket fetish. Every month or so she would end up back at the craft store and return with another adorable pattern to add to our collection.

We'd ordered food on the way home. I was feeling distinctly happier than I had all day. I kept logs in the fireplace all the time, just in case—but I was rarely angry enough at home to need them.

I put on the kettle for tea while Delia curled up with her laptop and two or three blankets, pulling up a British baking competition for us to watch once our food arrived. Alphonso—her fluffy black cat—yowled once and negotiated a place on her lap just before the doorbell rang, signaling the arrival of some poor delivery guy with our food.

I headed down the stairs, boots slipped back on, with a generous cash tip and a grumbling stomach.

I opened the door. "Hello?" I said, and then stopped.

It was not some poor delivery guy.

At first I thought it was no one at all. Then I saw the card—an oversized playing card floating in midair. My grumbling stomach dropped straight to my toes, clearing out that space for horror.

Fuck.

A gust of wind swirled the snow around the porch—giving edges to the outline of the thing that had found me.

It was shaped like person, with the card where its heart would be. Its mouth stretched dark and empty and it was taller than me, a hulking shadow in the snow. I could see through it. I felt more than saw when it reached for me, limbs made of air whistling and slicing through the night.

I stumbled back, hitting the stairs and putting a hand back to balance myself. A gust of wind kept the door open, and the *construct*—there's a word I hadn't thought of since I was a teenager, but that's absolutely what this thing was—the construct tried to come in after me.

Mercifully, my very old training kicked in. I popped back up and threw a punch, connecting with the almost-nothing. It felt like hitting a balloon—except this one stood its ground. I turned the punch into a shove, pushing the thing back out of the door and onto our icy porch.

I stepped out after it and, predictably, slipped—skidding down to one knee. Snow swirled around a loose formation of limbs and the construct's arms stabbed towards me, sharper than the cold air. I ducked and scrambled and put up a hand, focusing on the pain in my knee and my growing fury that this *thing* had come to my home.

I set the card that was the heart of the construct on fire.

It was hard—the magic of the construct resisted me, but I was furious and a tiny spark was all it took. The fire disrupted the magic holding the construct together. It vanished in a freezing puff of air. The card, which had animated it, floated down to fall singed and emptied of its magic beside me.

Shaking from the cold and the adrenaline, my knees soaked in melted snow, I picked up the ruined card.

It was good paper, thick and almost heavy in my hand. What was left of the back was painted in black and gold. I flipped over the card, dread surging. I stared at the half-burnt face of the Knight of Swords, one of the court cards of the tarot, and fought down nausea.

Now I had time to be really scared—more even than when I was fighting the construct. I knew, I'd always known, that someday the City would catch up with me. I didn't expect the Court of Swords to send assassins. This was not good.

"Hello?"

I looked up.

"You order Chinese?"

Our deliveryman stood at the bottom of the porch steps, understandably puzzled.

I stood up carefully, putting the tarot card in my pocket

and fishing out the cash for his tip.

"Yeah," I said. "Thanks."

I went back inside, carrying the paper bag with our hot food and trying to figure out what I was going to do next.

FOUR

Preparing for a Siege

TURNS OUT THAT WHAT I did next was change into pajamas and eat a ridiculous amount of noodles.

Once changed, I curled up with Delia on the couch with her laptop and her cat, and then we spent the evening the way we usually do on weekdays. I was jumpy, one ear listening for another knock at our door. Or for the door to be knocked in. Delia noticed, but I passed it off as just a worse day than normal. I was impatient for her to go to bed. I would not be sleeping much tonight. I needed to redo the wards on the house. And figure out how to ward the stupid office. That was going to be trickier.

Eventually Delia fell asleep on the couch. I woke her up and sent her to bed, along with a grumbling Alphonso—he didn't understand what could possibly warrant waking *him* up.

I checked the street outside, peering down at the

road—white with new snow—and didn't see anything lurking. Not that that made me feel much better. How the hell had they found me? And why now?

I'd escaped the magical Courts of the tarot and their City—their intrigues and their assassinations—a long time ago. Or I thought I had.

Most people think that tarot cards are superstitious nonsense—wiccans sometimes take them seriously, but for most folks it's a parlor trick. People are interested, the way they are in astrology, because it has to do with *them*. Who doesn't like talking about themselves and their future for awhile?

But they don't believe in them.

Like a lot of magic, the humans in the real world have the tarot all wrong.

Sideways of the real world, lurking in the light through stained glass windows, lanes that go to nowhere and the top floor of skyscrapers is the City. It's ruled by the living, breathing cards of the tarot. It's the most dangerous place in any world and it's where I was born.

The tarot is divided into two kinds of cards— the Major Arcana and the Minor Arcana. The Major Arcana are the ones you'll see in movies when a for-tuneteller is reading tarot cards—Death and the Fool and the Lovers, etc... They're dangerous and have the most power, but will usually leave you alone if you don't bother them. It would have been as foolish to hide from them as it would be to think they would care about finding me.

The Minor Arcana are mostly equivalent to the cards in a regular deck, but instead of hearts, diamonds, clubs and spades, the suits are cups, disks, wands and swords. Each has their element too: water, earth, fire, and air. The Houses of the Minor Arcana are endlessly at war with each other, and will happily kill you if you get in their way. Or because you've annoyed them. Each Suit and their House is ruled by a Court—a King, Queen, Knight, and Princess. The Courts are petty. They're selfish and they know how to hold a grudge.

My mother is the Queen of Wands.

∞

There are dozens of different ways to use tarot cards in magic—constructs like the one I'd just fought were one of them. Magical defenses—called wards—are another. Basic wards aren't complicated to do. I'd set tarot cards facing out from the house, infused with my magic and hidden in window frames and behind bookcases around the outer walls. They were all sevens of wands - a card that meant defense, its image showing one man fending off six attacking quarterstaves. I'd had to buy a dozen different decks to get all the sevens of wands that I needed— and to have spares besides. The extras were all shoved under my bed somewhere.

I'd kept wards up everywhere I lived since I'd left the City, but I didn't worry about them much after I'd set them. Now, I was worried.

I reached behind the couch to check the first card, flipping it over.

The image was smeared and charred.

Shit.

Someone had been trying to find me, had broken

through my wards, and I didn't how long our protection had been down.

I went to check the other cards. All of them had been destroyed. I hadn't noticed.

That's when I heard someone knocking on the door at the bottom of the stairs again.

I took a deep breath and got angry.

The Court of Swords had tried to hurt me—maybe even kill me—earlier. They sent constructs after me, to my home, where my best friend was sleeping. I was going to crisp the bastards, whatever they were.

Delia and I kept a bat by the door. I picked it up and went to see who it was this time.

FIVE

A Knight in a Three Piece Suit

I was expecting another construct on my doorstep. I was expecting my mother. I was expecting the Chinese delivery guy or the police. Instead, the man on my doorstep was a stranger—and a strange one at that.

He was tall, with hair that looked like burnished copper and a pale complexion. He wore a long dark red coat over a lanky frame. His eyes were pale blue and earnest. When I opened the door he immediately began to search my face—his expression a little raw, a little desperate. My first thought was that he had a face to be wary of. It was too honest. Too open. I didn't quite believe it.

"Are you Miss Charity Waits?" he asked. He had the faint accent of the City.

"I am. What do you want?"

"Oh," he said. "I'm the Knight of Wands. You're in

great danger, Miss Waits, and if you'll invite me in I can explain."

"I dealt with the danger and I don't want to talk to you or anyone to do with the Court of Wands. Go away."

I went to close the door. He caught it, concerned.

"You dealt with it? What did you deal with?"

"A construct. It's gone."

"What sort of construct?"

"Really, I don't need your help, Sir. Go away." The honorific slipped from me without thinking. I said 'sir' as easily as I would have had we met in the City. Infuriating. I tugged on the door again, but he wouldn't let go.

"Please, I have to talk to you, Miss Waits. You'll understand why, I promise, but please let me in."

"I said 'no' and if my mother thinks that all she has to do is send some *minion*—"

"It's about your mother."

"I don't want anything to do with her. And she bloody well knows that."

"Please—"

"Go away!" I yanked the door closed and he barely got his fingers clear. I could still see the top of his head through the window in the door.

"She's dead," he said, his voice muffled through the wood and the door of the glass.

I didn't understand him at first. I stood frozen with one hand on the door knob and the bat in the other.

He was still there.

She's dead.

My mother. That's what he meant.

I closed my eyes. *Damn her,* I thought.

Then came the guilt, followed fast by anger. She'd found a way to get me to talk to someone from the City again. She'd had to be dead to do it, but still. A fucking victory for her.

I opened up the door.

"Come in, sir," I said. "And be quiet. My roommate is asleep." *If my door slamming didn't wake her.*

"Thank you, Miss Waits," he said, mournful and worried. He smelled a little like a campfire and pine trees. "I'm so sorry for your loss."

I didn't answer. I closed and bolted the door behind him and then led him upstairs.

As soon as we were inside I turned to the fireplace, and my emergency stack of logs. I was angry enough that it took nothing at all to light them from across the room. I didn't even have to point. The Knight of Wands started and watched me, alarmed.

"Sit down," I said.

He took off his outer coat, folding it carefully and laying it over the back of the couch. He glanced around, curious, and gave me a chance to examine him too. Under a relatively ordinary coat, his clothing was almost fit for the human world—for a period tv show or something anyway. He wore a burnt orange cravat and a red vest embroidered heavily in gold. His cufflinks where wands. On his right hip, like a weapon, was a leather box—it would hold his tarot deck. On his left hip hung a short golden wand, like a scepter. That was his 'focus', and it would amplify his magic. I let out a breath, wishing that I had more than just my anger and my fire to defend myself.

He sat down, folding one long leg over the other.

He avoided my eyes, avoided looking at me at all. I'd remained standing in the middle of the room—between the couch and the fireplace. I didn't feel like sitting.

"Tell me how my mother died and why a construct came after me tonight."

"What sort of construct was it?" he asked.

"Swords," I said. "An air construct."

"It had a card in it?"

"Of course it did," I said. I fished in the pocket of my coat and handed him the half burnt card I'd saved. The Knight of Swords.

"He'll send more," said the Knight of Wands, concerned. "You were lucky to survive one."

"It wasn't hard," I said. Constructs are simple magical servants. I could have handled three or four with no more trouble, I was sure.

The Knight of Wands considered that and said, "Well, I suppose you are her daughter." Now he looked at me— but he was looking for *her*.

I made the logs behind me burned brighter.

"I came to bring you home," he said. "Gather what you want to bring and we'll go now."

"Absolutely not." I hissed it so that I wouldn't scream.

"The Court of Swords won't leave you alone, you know. You won't be safe here anymore."

"This is home," I told him. "And that's what the wards are for."

As I said that, Delia's cat made an appearance. He looked inquiringly at me, yellow eyes shining out of the shadows. Then he turned and stalked over to the Knight. The Knight put out a hand and Alphonso, never one to pass up the promise of affection, came forward and bumped his fluffy head against his extended hand.

"Yes," the Knight said, forehead creasing while he pet Alphonso's arching back, "I noticed. Why is your house warded against Wands? It took me longer than it should have to warn you because of those."

"I didn't want to be found," I said. "Now, what happened to my mother?"

A shiver ran through him while he decided what to tell me. "She was murdered," he said finally, sticking with the simple version. "Assassins. A Sword."

"Where?"

"What does it matter?" he asked.

"Was it in the palace?" I clarified.

"No. We're not sure where. Her body was left..." he stopped and I finally considered that he might have a good reason to be sparing me the details. This sounded bad.

"What was she doing?" I asked, "Out of the palace?"

"We don't know," he said. The pent up frustration in his voice made me want to step back. I didn't. When I was still in the City the Knight of Wands had been a old man. He'd been reckless—always pushing my mother towards a fight. He led every charge he could, and charged alone when no one was interested in following. My mother's favorite servant.

He must have died too, for there to be a new Knight of Wands.

This Knight was older than me, but I couldn't tell by how much. It could have been five years. Or ten.

While I was thinking about all this, the Knight recovered himself—but the anger over my mother's death was still there, under the surface.

"That's why you have to come with me," he said.

"No," I said.

He drew a breath, holding onto his temper as hard as I was holding onto mine. "It's my duty to keep you safe. She would have wanted that. You don't understand, Charity."

"I don't care. I'm not going."

"Your mother—"

"Was a monster."

He froze.

I felt guilty again, for saying it aloud and for the awful hurt in his face. As his shock retreated, I got another glimpse of his temper—but directed at me this time. His hand twitched and I thought—for a split second—that he would go for his deck or focus and incinerate me.

When he spoke again, his voice shook: "She's not—I didn't know, but she's not—" That was all he managed.

He stood up to leave, gathering his coat.

"Your mother," he said, his shakiness gone cold now. "My Queen. Was murdered by the Court of Swords. Now they want you too. You've got some power—to wield your magic in the mundane world—but they'll catch you unawares eventually. Or try something you don't suspect. You have this power because she *gave* it to you. She could have used that. Wands could use that. The City is the safest place for you. It's where you belong."

He reached into a vest pocket and drew out a tarot card. It was not a card from his personal deck, but an extra disposable card—like the one in the air construct. I braced myself, ready for magic again, but he just held the card out to me. I took it carefully—avoiding his fingers.

It was his card—a knight of wands painted in red and orange, horsed and in full armor. It had his face. His too kind eyes.

"Use that to summon me," he said. "If you change your mind."

SIX

In Which I, Like Pandora, Open a Box

I WATCHED THE KNIGHT OF Wands walk away from our house and turn left on the sidewalk before disappearing into the dark. I wondered what where he was crossing between the real world and the City. We lived out in a suburb because it would be further from anywhere that was easy. Delia didn't know that, of course, but it was a consideration I always had when we moved.

With care, I placed new cards.

I'd need to check them more frequently if the Courts were interested in me again, because my mother—

Damn it. Or, as they would say in the City: *World damn.*

I went to my room with Alphonso following me. He yowled, as though to ask why on earth I was up this late, intruding on his alone time. I scratched his fluffy black ears and knelt down by my desk. It took a minute of rooting around among the various boxes and bins I'd shoved under there over the last year, but I found my City box.

I took it out, blew the dust off the top and set it in the middle of my bed. Then I looked at it like it might bite me. Because it might. It's as close to Pandora's box as I have. Opening it had consequences.

The lid was painted with lacquer—marked with two crossed wands. It used to be kept closed with magic, but so long in the real world—the mundane world—had worn away at the spell. I didn't have the skill to recast the charm.

So I opened it like it was an ordinary box.

I didn't keep much when I left the City. A ring I never wore and a locket I never opened. A handful of cards, a small brass token shaped like a wand. A rose my father had given me.

And my deck. My living deck.

I picked it up, still in its leather case and felt the weight of the cards. It had been a long time and they were annoyed with me. They felt neglected. Which was fair. Aside from having opinions sometimes, a living deck was more powerful than an ordinary deck—and its art changed, reflecting its owner and the current state of the living tarot.

I popped open the case, the leather stiff and cracking.

I reached in and drew a card at random.

It was, of course, the queen of wands.

Like all the court cards, she sits alone—enthroned with a wand in her hand and her eyes glaring directly out of the card to meet my own. With my mother's face.

Like me, my mother was born in the City. She'd been

born into the House of Wands. Most people in the House served the Suit of Wands and its Court, but were not cards themselves. My mother's grandfather was the Eight of Wands, I think. She'd trained and practiced and been the strongest candidate to walk the Fool's Path when the old Queen of Wands died.

Positions in the Minor Arcana—the Suits—and their Courts aren't handed down. I was never the Princess of Wands, despite my mother's position. Those titles are earned—a numbered position is earned through service to the Suit, special training, and the approval or 'countenance' of certain Major Arcana. A place in the Court is earned by a series of trials referred to as the Fool's Path, meant to earn the countenance of *all* the Major Arcana. That countenance means that you can use their cards in magic to a certain extent—which makes for more powerful spells. My mother started grooming me to walk the Fool's Path before I was old enough to know what on earth she was talking about.

I might have already tried to earn a place in the Court, if I'd stayed. Perhaps as the Knight.

But my father was murdered.

I'd cried when he died. I felt like I should cry now too. Hate her as I did, my mother was dead. I should feel something.

I stared at her card and rolled the ring—a golden crown that fit over my thumb—around in my palm. The ring had belonged to my father. My mother had the other one.

He was another City native—an enchanter and builder in service to the Court of Wands. My mother got him killed. She used him as bait, used him because Swords assumed that she actually cared about her daughter's father—and would come to his rescue. She let them take him, let them kill him, and caught the Princess of Swords on her own.

The Queen of Wands considered it an obvious trade, like a move in a game of chess—her pawn for their princess. A no-brainer.

I put her card back in my tarot deck and closed the snap on the case, feeling the disgruntled weight of the cards. I was sorry, but I left it closed.

Alphonso jumped up on the bed with me, prowling around the box, sniffing, and deciding that it was clearly a bad idea.

He was right.

I packed the box back up and shoved it underneath my desk again.

Then I lay down, stretched out and stared at the ceiling. Alphonso settled, purring, on my chest and I pet him, knowing that if I slept, it would be despite myself.

SEVEN

Constructs and Coffee

NOTHING IS SO BAD THAT it can't get worse. I forget that sometimes, though never for long. The world doesn't let you, does it?

I zombied through my morning—Delia told me two or three times that I looked like death and should stay home. On the one hand, I should have listened to her. By noon I was barely keeping myself from nodding at my desk. In between adrenaline spikes, that was. Because on the other hand, if I had stayed home, the constructs might have hurt someone else. Or stormed our apartment.

The first of the constructs found its way into the break room. It cornered me while I was waiting for coffee to brew. At first I thought I was hallucinating. How the hell had it gotten inside? Who lets a floating tarot card into a business park?

It came for me, whooshing and stabbing out with long

tendrils of air. One caught my arm as I brought it up and pointed to the card controlling the construct. I burnt the card to cinders and the construct dissipated. I didn't leave any of the card to see who was controlling it this time. I was angry I hadn't had nearly enough coffee yet. Besides that, I'd arrived to an email from one of our suppliers—Mr. Saunders order was going to be delayed by two days. Because he'd forgotten to send it in the first place.

I was still staring at the pile of ashes, wondering if anyone would notice them, when Delia came in.

"Hello, chérie, is the coffee..." she stopped and followed my gaze. She poked the charred pile with the toe of her stylish boot. "What's this?"

"There when I got here," I said with a shrug, glad I'd completely destroyed the card.

Delia stared at it for a moment longer and then rolled her shoulders in an oh-well-not-my-problem way. It took me a moment to realized why that gave me shivers.

Delia and I had been friends for years. She'd occasionally been on the edge of discovering my supernatural hometown—she'd almost seen me set things on fire, she'd seen my box from the City, but not what was inside it. She'd been upstairs last night when the first construct showed up. She could have answered the door though.

I was confident that I could defend myself from the constructs, but Delia? Could I keep her safe too? At home and at work? I would have to.

"Are you alight? Seriously, kitten. I can take you home if you're feeling—" I waved her off.

"Really," I said. "Really, I'm okay."

She knew I was lying. She sighed heavily and put her

hands on my shoulders, looking directly into my eyes. "You know I love you, right honey?" I smiled and pushed her off.

"I know," I said. "Let me get a handle on it."

She nodded.

I poured her coffee and went to deal with Bellman and Saunders, with my mind entirely on other things.

I admitted to myself that I was putting Delia in danger.

I didn't realize until I sat back down at my desk that the construct had cut my arm—straight through the sweater. Fortunately, the sweater was black and the cut was small. The blood didn't show on the material.

The second construct found me in the basement. This one was bigger and not really trying to hold a human shape.

I was down there, digging through an old filing cabinet, when I heard the telltale sounds of wind in the stuffy space. I turned around to find a small, roughly humanoid cyclone with a card at its center. I put up an arm, with plenty of fury to fuel my magic—but it rushed forward, blowing out the fire I tried to summon and crashing into me and the filing cabinet behind me. Heavy as those bastards are, it went over and I fell hard, the corner of the cabinet digging painfully into my side.

The construct surrounded me and now was pressing me in, holding me inside itself and pulling the air away from me. I didn't realize that's what was happening until I tried to breath normally, and found there was nothing there. Mouth agape, my body refused to believe there was no air, my lungs sucked in on nothing. I was now both furious and panicky.

That's not really what the construct wanted to happen.

The card at the center of the construct burst into violent flames.

So did the files in the cabinet I'd been digging through—and all the files in two more cabinets.

The sudden heat behind me had me scrambling and gasping to the stairs fast, while the smoke alarms went off.

I made it back to the first floor in time to see my co-workers looking around, wondering if this was just a drill—and did they really have to go outside in this weather?

The phone on my desk rang.

I answered and found myself talking to the fire department. Did we actually have an emergency or was it a false alarm?

I told them we did have a fire, because while I wasn't sure what sort of damage fire in the filing cabinets could cause, I thought it probably wasn't worth the risk of returning myself to handle it—and having to call the fire department again.

People heard me and started to file outside, Mr. Bellman first among them.

Outside, waiting for them to let us back into the building, I had time to think about *how* bad this was. The first two constructs had been no trouble at all. The third almost killed me. I was much further out of my league than I thought.

Beside me, Delia talked to a co-worker I didn't know and stamped her feet to keep warm. I felt sick.

While we waited, I kept scanning the landscape for constructs.

After we'd stood outside for forty minutes—some of us without our coats—the firemen came to talk to Mr. Bellman. He, distressingly, cast a glare in my direction.

It was nearly quitting time when we'd all returned to the office. Most people packed up their things to leave—calling the last hour a wash. Delia caught my eye on the way to my desk and waved her keys in my direction. I smiled and nodded. I'd meet her outside.

I had my coat on and my scarf in my hands when Mr. Bellman yelled, "Charlene!"

I closed my eyes and started counting backwards from ten. I'd expended my rage on two constructs already today, and still felt like I could explode at any minute. Nothing was safe. Especially not fucking Bellman.

However.

I put on the scarf, kept on my coat and walked his office. It wasn't snowing tonight—just dark and grey the way winter nights are, the streetlights reflecting off the snow already on the ground. The clouds brought the night early and wind rattled his giant window.

"Charlene, do you have anything you want to tell me?"

"I'm sorry?"

"Do you have anything you'd like to *tell me*?"

"No... I'm sorry, Mr. Bellman. I don't know what you're talking about."

"I know you started that fire," he said it with the air of a television detective.

"I, what?" I asked. My voice went low, instead of high. A smarter man than Bellman might have noticed.

"You were in the basement—smoking—and you

started the fire. I heard you on the phone. No one else knew if it was a drill or not."

"I—,"

"Do you have any idea how much trouble you're in? I knew you had a bad attitude and were lacking when it came to the details, Charlene. But I didn't think you were stupid."

I closed my eyes to summon my patience. There wasn't any left.

"I don't smoke," I said.

"Yes, you do," he said.

"I don't smoke," I repeated, and now my voice had found its angry, saccharine sweetness. "I take smoke breaks to get away from you. And your fucking tedious ineptitude."

"Why— You will—"

The wind gusted harder outside. The window buckled. I looked outside, squinting to try to see through the reflection from the light inside the room.

"... I will be writing you up, immediately. I'm disappointed! I'm shocked! I expect—"

There was a construct outside—the biggest yet.

The glass flexed and broke.

I was thrown back against the wall. Mr. Bellman flew into his desk.

A swirl of wind reached around me, lifting me. Air held me up beside the construct's face. It didn't speak— they can't—but I heard, very distinctly, a cold voice say: "You really aren't worth the trouble, Charity Waits."

I couldn't have agreed more. I wished these Swords bastards hadn't taken the trouble.

It squeezed me, crushing my ribs with a terrible, even, and inexorable pressure. I reached for the anger, but it slipped away from me.

I couldn't get a breath. I couldn't point my hand at the construct's card. I wasn't angry. I was surprised and caught off guard. I was being killed and I knew it. I was afraid. My body was preoccupied with trying to breath and it couldn't remember how to catch anything on fire.

You were lucky to kill one, I heard the Knight of Wands tell me.

Only the weak rely on luck. That one was my mother.

I gritted my teeth, thinking of her.

Rage burned through me and the card ignited in a fast bright firework of light.

I fell as the construct dissipated, landing awkwardly on the side of one ankle, and rolling down to the floor. I didn't move for a minute, enjoying the feeling of air rushing into my bruised body. Freezing air from the broken window, but still wonderful. I stood up.

After another few deep breaths, I walked around to where Mr. Bellman cowered under his desk. I pointed to his dead plants and all of them burst into merry flames.

"I quit," I said, then left the office.

I got looks from my ex-co-workers as I left. I'm sure the glass breaking and the sound of me hitting the floor had caught their attention. However no one had come to check on me, and I was confident that any account Bellman gave would make him sound crazy. I got out the door and stomped my way through the slush, to where Delia was waiting for me—the heat on and the ice cleared off the car.

I got into the passenger's seat and sat very still.

"Oh, kitten," said Delia, when she saw me. "You've *got* to tell me what's wrong."

She reached over to squeeze my hand, waiting with concern in her big brown eyes.

"My mom died," I told her, and finally burst into tears.

EIGHT

Going Away, Going Home

I DIDN'T TELL DELIA ALL of it, of course. There are some things—like constructs and magic—that are hard to explain at the best of times, let alone when you're a sobbing wreck of a human being.

She never asked me why I hadn't told her immediately. She didn't ask me what had happened—she told me I could tell her, of course. She knew that I didn't get along with my mother, so I didn't have to explain how conflicted I felt about her death. I didn't tell Delia my mother had been murdered or about the Court of Wands.

I did tell her I needed to go home for awhile—funeral arrangements and all that.

"Do you want company, kitten?" she asked. "I could come with you?"

"No," I said, even though having her there would have been marvelous. "No, I really don't want anyone else to have to deal with her... family. Seriously. I'll be better off alone."

"Then I can help cover for you here? So Mr. Bellman doesn't fuss about the time off?"

Oh.

I told her I'd quit.

"You what?"

"You'll probably hear about it tomorrow. Mr. Bellman accused me of setting the fire earlier. And I quit."

That was close enough for now. Delia roundly abused him as an idiot for a few minutes. It made both of us feel better.

"But—and I know you hate working for him—but do you want to quit? I'm sure, with your mother and all, that he'll have to take you back if you explain..."

I shook my head.

"I don't want to do it any more, Delia. I'll find a way to pay rent."

She nodded. She wasn't worried about that part.

"Then what can I do?" she asked.

"Help me pack?" I asked, sniffing and wiping my face. "And drive me to the airport?"

"You sure you don't want me to come in?" Delia asked, the car in park outside of departures at the airport. I shook my head.

"I've got awhile to wait before my plane leaves," I said. "I'll be back in a few days at the latest. Don't worry about me."

Delia laughed. She was going to worry.

I got out and got my suitcase from the trunk. Then I checked for constructs, but everyone at Cleveland Hopkins Airport was human enough. Delia got out of the car to give me a final hug and I held onto her a little long. I was going to miss her, even if it was only going to be a few days.

I kept telling myself that. I'm nothing if not brilliant at self-delusion.

"Text me?" asked Delia. Her eyes looked damp.

"Of course," I said, and hoped I could from the City.

She nodded too fast and got back in the car.

I walked in through the automatic doors, my suitcase rolling behind me, and glanced back to see Delia's brake lights release, and then watch her disappear.

I gave Delia a minute to get on the road and then went down an escalator—from departures to arrivals. I went back outside, my breath misting in the cold air in front of my face and eyed a line of taxis.

I took out the card the Knight of Wands had given me.

I would go to the City and make a deal—something to protect Delia and I from the Court of Swords. Then I would come home. A few days would be plenty.

"I changed my mind," I told the card and held it in my ungloved hand. It got hot, immediately, but thankfully didn't burst into flames.

The automatic doors opened behind me, and I turned to see the Knight of Wands in his dark red overcoat walking towards me.

"Miss Waits," he said, and picked up my suitcase. "Let's go home."

NINE

Carousel

"THAT WAS QUICK," I said, following the Knight of Wands into the airport.

He looked left and right at the luggage carousels, then headed away from the busy ones to an empty few at the far end of the arrival hall.

"You stayed," I said, as we walked. "You didn't go back to the City. Between now and when we spoke."

He glanced over his shoulder and down at me. "No, why would I?"

"Because I wasn't going to come back to the City."

"You were being attacked," he said, actually confused. "I didn't get all of them, I'm sorry about that—but I couldn't let you fight them alone. She wouldn't have—" He stopped and faced an empty carousel.

I shivered. "I destroyed three. How many did you take care of?"

43

"More," he said.

"Right."

I'd known I was in over my head. Now I was seeing exactly how far in. I didn't like it. At least it was nice to know my decision to go to the City for help was the right one. Sort of nice.

"What are we using to get there?" I asked. I'd expected us to hop in a taxi and head for downtown. Getting to the City wasn't difficult. It just took an enormous amount of power and a landmark in the real world with an echo in the City. So I'd expected him to take us to the nearest convenient location that had a counterpart in the City.

"This," he said, still staring intently at the empty luggage carousel. He handed me back my suitcase.

The Knight reached under his coat and drew out a tarot card. I caught a quick glimpse of the eight of wands— eight staves flying through the air over a summery field.

He held out the card and put out his other hand to me.

"Ready?" he asked, without turning away from the card and the empty space beyond it.

I took his hand. He stepped carefully around the luggage carousel to the left, circling it counterclockwise and pulling me with him. We must have seemed mad.

As we came around the end of the carousel, I felt the world bend. It had been a long, long time. It was like going on a rollercoaster for the first time as an adult. Reflexively, I held onto him harder.

I didn't see the change—I was preoccupied by the way my stomach was suddenly flying all over the place, on the need to put one foot in front of the other and on his hand, which had become the anchor point for my existence.

Then we were through—and standing in a different airport.

"What..." I said, but couldn't find the words.

The only sound was the soft whir of escalators and the luggage carousels turning slowly, empty. The different floors were open to each other and I was able to walk to a balcony and look up to empty railings above me and down to departure counters. It was a ghost airport.

Across from me was a wall of glass. Beyond the white plastic seats, polished steel railings and glass was a mostly empty sky, with only a few too bright stars visible.

Under those bright stars—far away, with a gulf of darkness between us—was the City. Behind me, the Knight said, "The number of high tech airports in the mundane world has increased dramatically—it made sense to pull this one to the City, in order to travel to the mundane world. Easy to get to a lot of places."

When I first saw a photo of the Shanghai skyline, I thought it looked like a human had glimpsed the City, and tried to replicate it in the munda— in the real world.

It appeared to be a human city and *not*. Strange silhouettes of improbable buildings—some recognizable, none of which belonged there—all stared back at me, built with undeniable stability in an improbable jumble.

"There are no planes... just the airport?" I was trying to follow what the Knight had told me.

"Why would there be planes?" he asked.

"Because it's an airport..." I said, like an idiot.

He dropped my hand. I'd forgotten we were holding hands.

"How do we get there?" I asked.

"There's a train," said the Knight of Wands and, taking my suitcase again, he led the way. I paused for a second to check my phone. It was scrambled—no signal and the screen itself flickered and danced.

"I'm sorry, Delia," I whispered. It really would need to be only a few days.

TEN

The Train at Twilight

THE PEOPLE OF THE CITY don't like to lift things exactly as they are from the real world—they like a hodgepodge, an eclectic mix. You would not mistake the airport in the City for a real one. Or the train. The escalator we took down to reach the train curved into the shape of a spiral staircase, turning us around and around as we went past empty floor after empty floor.

After the first glimpse of the City's skyline, I tried not to look at it. Part of it, surprisingly, felt a bit like home. I hated that.

We dropped below ground on the spiral escalator and followed signs through a network of broad, empty hallways to the train. Signs for arrivals, departures, and food-courts all led to nothing and frequently contradicted each other. In multiple languages.

I followed the Knight and tried to think about what I

would say to the King. That's who I was going to need to convince to help me. I was going to need to be specific about my requests.

In the courts of the tarot, the King and the Queen are equal—but their roles are different depending on which Court you are in. Usually—usually, mind you, because if ever there was a place where every rule has an exception, it's the bloody City—the Queens dominate the politics of Swords and Wands, while the Kings focus on magic. It's the other way around for Cups and Disks— the Queens wield the greater magic while the Kings conduct the politics.

I thought the King would probably be the one I knew when I was a kid, he walked the Fool's Path a year or so before I left. I didn't know him well then—why would I?—but I did have a vague recollection of him: a craggy face. Grumpy. His focus was black stone, like obsidian, shaped as a scepter. I remembered that because it was odd. Most of the Court of Wands use gold and wood for their instruments—I could not remember seeing another one made of black stone in all my childhood.

When we reached the train platform—passing through five different sorts of unguarded barriers, that all opened when we approached without the need for tickets—a train composed of a dozen slightly different subway cars awaited us. Through the windows though, instead of plastic seats and florescent lights, I could see wood paneled interiors with plush armchairs. The Knight lead us inside, and set my suitcase on a polished wooden shelf before sinking into one of the armchairs with a relieved sigh.

The doors closed behind us, and the train started to

move immediately. We were the only ones in the car. I took the armchair next to his.

"How," asked the Knight of Wands, "Do you stand living in the mundane world? It's so— grating."

"What? You mean it all makes sense?" I said.

"I mean your magic—it beats you down to be out there. To have it all crushed into you... like a difference in gravity."

"You were born in the City?" I asked.

"Of course," he said, mildly offended.

I nodded and turned my attention to the window. We were underground and we zipped by stations that were each somewhere different in the real world—except these were empty. We were still in a ghost world, all this called into being because it was convenient to walk around a luggage carousel and go wherever you wanted. It made everything feel late, like it was 3am and we kept getting lucky to see the platforms entirely empty.

"Forgive me," said the Knight. "I know you choose to live in the mundane world, and must have found something to love in it. But I—I've never stayed there for more than a few hours before now, and the last few days have been uncomfortable."

"It's fine," I said. His hair was a blonde-ish orange in this light, and he was less pale and tense than he had been sitting in my living room. The clothes were just as ridiculous, of course, but they seemed more natural in this setting too. My t-shirt and jeans were the costume out of place, as opposed to his gold cufflinks and embroidered three-piece suit.

"This seems like it's the long way to get to the Palace of Wands," I said.

"It wouldn't be safe to arrive too close to the Palace," he said.

"Why?"

"Wards," he answered. "We'd be killed by our own defenses."

"Was it always like that?" I asked. I thought I could remember being able to walk through to the mundane—the real world right outside the gates of the Palace of Wands.

"No," he said. "But it has been so for a long time."

"Since I left?"

"About then, I suppose," said the Knight, carefully. I was missing something there. Worth remembering. "We are almost at open war with Swords."

I thought we'd always been at war with Swords, but didn't say so.

"And Cups? Disks?"

"They've had their own spats and squabbles—and sometimes have helped us or Swords, but they've not committed in a way that's tipped our war. Disks lost a few cards to a game with the Devil a few years back, but that was the most dramatic conflict they've dealt with in awhile. They are almost recovered."

The Devil was a Major Arcana—one of the greatest dangers in the City. One that I hoped I never ran into. One *everyone* hoped they didn't run into. That one and the Tower are the surest signs your life is about to suck.

"How did they get to my mother?" I asked.

She didn't take risks, my mother. She didn't make mistakes.

"We don't know," said the Knight, soft and apologetic.

50

He leaned forward in his armchair, fingers interlaced and looking at me with concern. Looking at me like my mother had died.

"Meaning?" I said. I'd had my cry over her death with Delia. I was back to thinking about her as the monster she is. Was.

"She was left at the gate—it must have taken a strong enchantment to keep us from seeing who. We don't know why she was out there. She'd been—" he stumbled, and I almost told him that it didn't bother me to talk about it, when I realized it bothered *him*. He was grieving more for my mother than I was.

"You liked her," I said.

He swallowed. "She was my queen," he said, and then: "I let her die. I'm sorry."

"My mother," I said carefully, "Did whatever she wanted. Whatever she was doing out there alone, she did it because that's how she thought it should be done. No one could have told her otherwise."

He bowed his head over his hands.

The surreality of the situation hit me hard then, sitting on a train that went between an airport and a city that would never use it, in a subway car with plush armchairs with a crying supernatural knight.

I only knew he was crying when I saw a tear fall from his face onto the thick carpeting.

I opened my mouth, searching for something more to say—but I didn't know him, or what might comfort him. More importantly, I didn't know the *her* that the Knight had lost.

Tentatively, I put a hand on the back of his hunched

shoulder, smoothing the fabric of his red overcoat in what I hoped was a soothing manner. We stayed like that and didn't speak again until the train arrived in the City.

ELEVEN

Shadow on the Roof

THE TRAIN ONLY STOPPED at the station we wanted—I suppose the City does have its advantages.

The Knight looked up and his face was dry. He took my suitcase and said, as we stepped onto a platform elevated above the street, "I don't think Swords will try anything—but keep your eyes open."

We stepped out onto the platform—and were met by an honor guard. I froze, one foot still on the train and then rapidly unfroze when the doors began to hiss shut behind me. Six guards—men and women—in trim red and orange uniforms with gold braid at their shoulders and gold buttons down their chest came to attention in unison.

"Are you ready, Miss Waits?" asked the Knight, offering me his arm. I took it, because the unfamiliar knight was abruptly more familiar than anything else.

The guards fell in around us.

Following the bizarre near solitude of the airport and the train, the lightly peopled station seemed crowded.

I was uncomfortable in my puffy jacket and scarf, because they stood out and because both were unnecessary—it felt more like autumn in the City than winter. My jeans were the only pair in sight. Beyond the guards were men and women in everything from renaissance garb to kimono to three piece suits, from ballgowns to artful rags. It felt like Halloween—one where I stood out because I'd forgotten to dress up.

On the bright side, people got out of our way.

Our party moved down the stairs to street level and onto the sidewalk of the City. It was wider than in most human cities—pedestrians and rickshaws making up the majority of the traffic. Trucks and cars were rare, and weren't really trucks and cars to begin with—they were magical constructions, relics with the veneer of modernity like the train or the buildings. It was magic and illusion and power that held the City together, not mechanics.

We walked past shops that would have been at home in a dozen different cities—that probably *borrowed* from a dozen different cities. This wasn't the sleek glass and steel I'd been able to see from the airport. These buildings were only a few stories high, brick and stone for the most part. Great trees lined the street, their branches bare and skeletal.

If all that wasn't enough to tell me I was in the City, there were the symbols. The ones on our guard's uniforms were obvious—their colors and the embroidered golden wands on their backs and on the cases for their tarot decks and the shapes of the clubs hanging from their belts all proclaimed their allegiance. Most of the City was more subtle.

Hidden in every shop window, twisted into wire bracelets and necklaces, in umbrella handles, in the decorative cobblestones under my feet, in tattoos and in neon and in handprinted calligraphic signs were symbols declaring loyalty to different suits and to the Major Arcana. Wands predominated the area, of course, but I saw Disks too and a good number representing The Sun and Strength.

While taking it all in, I looked up and caught sight of someone sitting on a roof's edge—their feet dangling over the street. I couldn't see them well—they were simply a silhouette, but I thought they were watching me. They raised a hand and waved.

Distracted by the figure, I almost missed the gate to the Palace of Wands.

The Palace of Wands is a slightly misleading name. It's not a single building, but rather a sprawling collection of buildings—all surrounded by a high white stone wall. The gate is wrought iron cast in the shape of a hundred crisscrossed wands, their details picked out in gold leaf. More guards—in even more ornate dress—stood to either side of the gate.

They bowed to us as we approached and then opened the gate for us.

"Welcome home, Miss Waits," said one of our entourage, surprising me.

"Thank you," I managed.

Inside the gates, bowls of fire lit the walkways, looking for all the world like a very fancy medieval college campus. I didn't find it familiar. Seven or so years can change a lot of geography in the City, but it still felt strange to not recognize anything at all in the Palace of Wands.

The Knight took one of the paths, heading to the left. "I'm sorry," he said. "The King will want to see you immediately. I'm sure you'd rather rest, but he won't wait. It doesn't have to take long—" I followed him, leaving our escort behind at the gate.

"It's fine," I said.

He glanced back at me.

"I suppose it's very different?"

"It's changed," I said.

"Do you—" he stopped.

"Do I what?"

"It doesn't matter," he said. "This way."

He took us to a grand stone building—one with marble steps and an open atrium—lit from the inside now that it was night. He took us through another quick twist of corridors and I realized that finding my own way out of here, let alone back to the train, would be tricky. Of course, what could I do if I did make it back to the airport? I didn't know how to use my tarot deck to travel and there were no flights.

We approached a large set of closed sliding glass doors. To their left was a more ordinary office door. The Knight ducked his head into the office—I caught a glimpse of tapestries and more wood. That must be fashionable in the City right now, given the train car.

"Is he in?" the Knight asked someone. I craned my neck to see who.

Glancing up from her desk was a middle-aged woman

with her hair pulled into a tight black bun on top of her head. She looked exhausted.

"Yes, in the Garden," said the tired woman. She noticed me.

"This is her?"

"Yes, Miss Charity Waits, may I introduce the Ten of Wands?"

"Oh," I said. The woman—the Ten—stood up and moved gingerly around her desk, extending a hand. She wore a floor length black coat buttoned over a blood red blouse. I shook her hand. I thought she was the same Ten I'd known, but could not be sure.

"We're glad you're safe, Miss Waits. Welcome home. I'm sorry it's under such circumstances."

I started to say that it was fine, stopped myself and said: "Thank you."

She wore two little pins—bunches of five wands—one on each of her lapels.

"Her room is ready," said the Ten to the Knight, "When he's done with her." The Ten took my suitcase from the Knight. I almost protested, but let it go. I was in their hands as it was. No point pretending I had a whole lot of control right now.

"Thank you, Ten," said the Knight with slight courtly bow. Then he ushered me through the glass doors and into a desert.

TWELVE

The King of Wands

THE GLASS DOORS LED TO a great biodome. Lights from the floor turned the rectangular plastic sections of the dome white and opaque, the air was dry and the earth was sandy and golden. Desert plants—flowering cacti and small trees—lined the walkway. Little signs named the different plants in both English and what looked like Chinese to me.

A short walk brought us to a kind of balcony overlooking a wide stone courtyard in the midst of the biodome. It, in turn, was dominated by a fire pit and a large wooden seat. A throne.

Beside it stood the King of Wands.

He was the King I remembered—sharp featured, like he was carved by an impatient mason. He was younger than I'd thought though—anywhere between five and ten years older than me. In contrast to the Knight's finery and even the Ten's, he wore a black turtleneck and

58

olive slacks, with a gold circlet peering out of messy dark brown curls.

Next to the throne was a small table, and on that an arrangement of tarot cards. The King stared at the cards, engaged in finding some meaning there, so we stayed on the balcony for a moment.

Thinking about the guards that met us, I asked: "Is anyone allowed out of the Palace without an escort?" I spoke softly so as not to disturb the King.

"No," said the Knight. "Not since the Queen."

"It's really that bad?"

The Knight sent me a quick frown. I'd disappointed him again. "Yes," he said. "It's that bad."

"Have they attacked directly?"

"Not yet, but Swords will try it soon. With the Court so weakened."

Below us, the King frowned and then scooped up his cards—apparently done with his magic. A lazy hand came up and beckoned us down to his courtyard. He appeared tired too, and distracted.

The Knight took us down a staircase, and when we turned to see the King again, he'd seated himself in the throne—wood and banded metal with no cushion.

The Knight stayed back by the large bonfire and gestured me forward when I hesitated with him. I was suddenly nervous. Whether I liked it or not, the King of Wands wielded power. Things would go better if I was polite.

"We welcome you to the Court of Wands, Charity Waits," said the King. "I can see that you are indeed as powerful as your mother said you would be. We are pleased to sponsor you on the Fool's Path."

It took me a minute to realize what he was saying. When it clicked I was... displeased. The Fool's Path is the series of rites and rituals to earn the approval of the Major Arcana—the right to use their cards in magic—and become a Court Card. That was not why I was here.

"Excuse me?" I asked.

"We welcome you to the Court of Wands, Charity—" he started the whole thing again and I interrupted him.

"I meant," I said. "That I have no intention of walking the Fool's Path. Thanks and all, but no."

"Your mother always intended for you—"

"I could not care less what she intended." I said, fury already hovering—the fire wanting to get out.

The King looked at me, truly, for the first time.

"Is that so?" he rose. He was shorter than I remembered too, not as tall as the Knight, but he still managed to be menacing. "Well then. I, like her I'm sure, do not care what *your* intentions are. You are here. And I've need of a *Fool*. You'll do."

"You can't make me—"

"Of course I can," said the King of Wands.

This time I got a glimpse of him, the real him—the Court Card and enchanter. He wore such stately dress that he could barely move—his raiment embroidered with lions, and the staff he held, the wand, burned with power. He towered in fire and dignity. It hurt to look at him.

I blinked and we were back in the desert biodome, me in my jeans and him in his slacks.

"You don't want an unwilling Fool," I said, hoping it was true, trying to stay calm and reasonable. "I'll die on the Path. No help to you at all."

"You're too stubborn to kill yourself to spite me," the King said. "Or even to spite her."

I tried to catch my breath and failed.

"I came—" I started and then stopped, and lowered my voice from the half-yell, I'd started at. I focused on not setting his chair alight and spoke with warning sweetness. "I came for your help, Majesty. If you cannot help me, then I respectfully take my leave. If you try to keep me here against my will, I will do my best to make your life more miserable than it is now. And if I ever walk the Path, and gain the power of a court card, you can be damn sure you will not like how I use that power."

"I understand," said the King. He didn't. He clearly didn't. He also didn't care. "But my position is untenable and I must use the tools at my disposal."

I choked on his words—*at his disposal, what the fuck?*—rage threatened to overwhelm me. It was going to need to go somewhere.

"I am not your tool," I managed to say, "and what I want—"

"You are my subject," he said, shaking his head. He still seemed distracted. Like destroying my life wasn't even the most important thing on his fucking mind. The King continued: "What you want doesn't matter right now."

I lost control of my magic—I barely had time to redirect the fire from the King to a nearby tree.

The ensuing fireball threw me into the air and I didn't remember hitting the ground.

THIRTEEN

Burnt

"MISS WAITS," SOMEONE WAS SAYING. "Can you hear me?"

"It's Charity," I said.

"Oh," said the Knight of Wands and I opened my eyes.

I blinked, trying to bring the world into focus. The first thing I saw was the plastic panels that made up the ceiling of the biodome. I couldn't have been out for more than a minute because the air was still hotter than it had been. Or was that just me? I flinched. My body felt sunburned on one side.

"What happened?" I asked, focusing on the Knight with some difficulty.

"That's more properly a question for you," said the King somewhere behind the Knight. He said something else and a third person I could not see answered him.

I tried to sit up, found it was harder than I thought it was going to be and found the Knight of Wands picking me up and setting me on my feet. I let go of him fast and almost fell over again. He saved me from falling into a cactus and held me up with an irritated sigh.

Embarrassed, I said, "Thank you."

He arched one sandy eyebrow. "You're welcome."

That's when I got a look at my handiwork. I'd burnt half the biodome—the trees and pathways were blackened, the cacti shriveled. Fire had eaten the top and one side of the king's throne. White ashes fluttered in the air and everything smelt of smoke. I felt sick.

"Did I...?" I gestured at the destruction.

"Yes," said the King, marching towards me. I had his full attention now. I regretted wishing for it.

"I'm sorry," the words bubbled out, I was still shocked. "I didn't—that usually starts a little fire, like in a fireplace. Or one plant. Or a pallet or something. I didn't know that—what happened? Did I—shit, did I hurt anyone?"

"Hurt the King of Wands with fire?" asked the Knight. "You're strong, but that's not exactly easy."

"I meant—oh," I said.

"No. You didn't hurt anyone. Only yourself," said the King.

"It... why did I do so much damage?"

"Magic," the King said, speaking very slowly, "is more powerful in the City."

"Right," I said. *Shit.*

"You are apparently quite strong—exercising your magic in the mundane world has given you a surprising amount of raw power. However, you have no control at all."

"It just happens when I'm angry." Next to me, the Knight stiffened.

"It just..." the King shook his head in disbelief. "You've tied your magic to your temper?"

"I don't know what you mean."

"You... you only use magic when you're angry?"

"Sort of," I said. "The fire part anyway."

The King drew in his own furious breath and said, cold and scornful: "That is unbelievably stupid."

I swallowed and looked at the ruined garden.

"I apologize, Your Majesty," I said.

He stared at me for a long moment. I tried not to lean too much on the Knight of Wands, but I was exhausted and empty, my legs shook and my skin hurt where I'd burnt myself.

The King put the tips of his fingers to his forehead—an elegant facepalm.

"Goodnight, Miss Waits," said the King, gesturing for us to leave.

"Goodnight, Your Majesty," I said in chorus with the Knight.

The Knight of Wands walked hunched over to keep an arm under mine—still keeping me from falling. I wished I didn't need it, but not a lot to be gained by pretending I didn't.

We walked through the charred wreck of the biodome, past the wasteland my fireball had created and I tried to swallow the guilt. It wasn't real—nothing here had taken any time to grow, the King or someone had brought it into existence, an echo from the real world. But that work takes time and attention and love too. It's what my father had done here. I felt awful.

When we were out of the sliding glass doors, I caught

a glare from the Ten, who was coming out of her office, deck in hand—no doubt to help clean up my mess.

We stumbled on, heading for the exit. I felt the Knight shaking. I realized, late, that he was trying not to laugh.

"What is it?" I asked.

He kept chuckling.

"It's just... you only use magic when you're angry? That's..."

"Unbelievably stupid?" I said.

"Well, yes. I've never heard of anything like it. What in the World made you do it?"

"It seemed right," I said, struggling to explain my logic. I hadn't had any serious magical training since I was a teenager—and that had been my mother showing me things when she felt like it. "It's fire, right? It's angry."

He threw back his head and laughed louder.

"What?" I asked, bristling.

"It's like you took the stereotype about Wands and made it true!" he said. "It's like a joke. Wands can't keep their temper and Cups cry all the time. That sort of thing. And you don't even want to be a Wand."

"Oh," I said.

He kept laughing. I couldn't be too annoyed at not getting the joke. He had a nice laugh.

FOURTEEN

In Which We Make a Deal Over Breakfast

TOGETHER THE KNIGHT OF WANDS and I made our way across the grounds of the Palace of Wands to a different building—it was one that looked more like a European palace. He offered to carry me at one point and I'm ashamed to say I almost accepted the offer—I was that tired and there were stairs. I hardly noticed what the bedroom looked like. The bed was large and comfortable and as soon as the Knight left, I scrambled under the covers and fell asleep fully clothed.

The next morning, I woke up panicked from a nightmare where I was stuck in the Wands' throne room. No matter where I turned, I found myself facing the thrones—seats carved from orange and pink stone to resemble flames. In the dream, I turned away and away from the thrones, faster and faster and all to no avail.

Unfortunately, this particular nightmare didn't go

away entirely when I woke up. I was in the City with the Wands—and the King and I hadn't exactly gotten off to the best start.

I rolled out of bed and took in the room now that I had the energy to do so.

It was modern and sterile in a way that I hadn't seen yet in the City—like a fancy hotel room, all black and white and silver. My suitcase was lying across the bench at the foot of the bed. I got up and investigated the rest of the room. There was a tv—but it had no wires coming out of the back, so really it was more like a black picture in a black frame. I found one empty closet and one that was full of clothing that suited the City—gowns and jackets and fancy dress. There was a bathroom too, with an enormous shower.

That, I decided, was next.

I showered, wincing as the water hit my burnt skin. Later, a quick inspection in the mirror showed me that the burns weren't bad—my face was pinker than normal, but that was it—and I had a batch of bruises forming on my side and back.

I changed into clothes I'd brought with me from home. I choose jeans again and a comfortable blue top. I'd brought a half dozen outfits, some books, and my City box with me. I hadn't planned on staying very long. Still didn't.

In among the fancy clothes, I'd seen a belt meant to let me carry my tarot deck. I left it and my deck where they were.

I was wondering what to do next when someone knocked on the door.

"Come in," I called.

Someone new stuck their head in, a young woman with frizzy blonde hair. She came all the way into the room, revealing that she wore the livery of a servant of the Court of Wands.

"Good Morning, Miss Waits," she said with a curtsy. "I'm Rosette and I've been asked to see to you while you settle in."

"Oh," I said. Me at my most articulate.

"The Knight would like to know if you are receiving guests? Or will you join him for breakfast?"

"Breakfast sounds good, if you'll show me where it is," I said.

Rosette bowed to me. "Of course—if you're ready?"

"I suppose I am," I said.

She took me to the breakfast room. I had to laugh about the name. Of course, the Palace of Wands had a room specifically for breakfast. It probably had two or three. The Knight of Wands waited for me. He wore a pale orange shirt with a pink vest and pants—nearly as fancy as the suit he'd worn in the real world. It should have clashed with his hair, but it didn't. I wondered if he ever dressed casually.

He glanced up, saw *my* clothes and frowned, "You didn't like any of the things in your closet?" he asked. I thought he sounded a tiny bit wounded.

"I didn't know they were for me," I lied.

"Oh—yes, so you have something suitable for your time here. Until you can order your own things."

I opened my mouth to argue with him over the assumption that I would be staying long enough to 'order my own things', but the bacon smelled good, I hadn't had any coffee and I felt like earning my name a bit this morning. Plus, I still felt bad about the biodome.

The breakfast was served as a buffet, and I went to see what was waiting for me, I asked, "When do I get to meet the Princess?" The last of the Court of Wands, since my mother was gone and I'd now met the other two.

The Knight didn't answer, and I turned in time to see a hint of pain lingering on his features. My stomach dropped.

"I'm sorry," I said. "I don't... Why was that the wrong question?"

"There is no Princess of Wands," he said. "I thought you knew. The throne has been vacant for a time. Your mother... I think that perhaps she hoped that you would join the Court."

With the Court so weakened, he'd said the night before.

"She was keeping a spot on the Court open for me?"

"Not *keeping* it open," he said, covering for her.

"If so, that was a terrible plan," I said.

I'd offended him. "Whatever you thought," he said, cold, "She was a brilliant Queen. If you were her blind-spot, she wasn't the first parent to have that affliction."

It shouldn't have hurt, but it did.

"She should have filled the position," I said. "She knew I wasn't coming back. I made that very clear."

"And yet, here you are." The King of Wands entered the breakfast room, wearing a regal dressing robe, brown curls tousled.

"Majesty," I said, nervous.

"Miss Waits," he replied. "I don't feel like we've got-

69

ten off to a very good start. Perhaps we can seek our better selves this morning?"

"Sure," I said.

The King nodded to the Knight and got himself toast and black coffee before choosing a chair to lounge in.

I filled my plate and took a place at the table.

"How are you feeling this morning?" asked the King. "Not angry?"

"This is going to be a thing," I said, "Isn't it?"

"I doubt you'll ever live it down," said the King, perfectly serious.

"Great," I said, but I was relieved that he seemed to have forgiven me.

"I've given our predicament some thought, and I have a proposition for you, Miss Waits," said the King, munching on a slice of toast for all the world like he wasn't one of the most powerful enchanters in a city of enchanters.

"Oh?" I said, and took a gulp of coffee. I was clearly going to need it.

"You're here for my help, yes?" he said. "What do you want?"

"For Swords to leave my life in the real world alone."

"The real world?" he frowned.

"The mundane world," I said.

"Ah," he rolled his eyes. "As you like. Good, I can make that work. Here is my predicament: I need a Queen and a Princess as quickly as possible, and Wands has no one on the Fool's Path right now. It will take time to find proper candidates. During that time, Wands is especially vulnerable. If it seems like we've already found a Fool, and a powerful one, Swords is less likely to risk an open war. Which Wands would almost certainly lose."

The Knight looked pained, but did not contradict him.

I nodded to show I was following.

"Now, you are right that I don't want an unwilling Fool. I frankly don't have the strength to fight with both you and Swords, Miss Waits. Exhausting. Still, until we show them another candidate—or better yet, two candidates—Swords are going to assume you *will be* the candidate and therefore a threat to them. You aren't going to convince them otherwise. So. What I propose is this:

"You stay here and pretend to be reacquainting yourself with the City in preparation for walking the Fool's Path—that reads, no one expects you to leap onto the Path. Meanwhile, I will find another suitable candidate—this will arouse no suspicions since there are two empty places in the Court. Once I have my candidate, you may return to your 'real world' and I will do my best to see that you aren't bothered there."

I thought about it, trying to find the trick and reminding myself that all the Court of Wands are manipulative bastards.

"I can think about it?"

The King shrugged elegantly. "Certainly, if you think about it here in the palace. While reacquainting yourself with the House of Wands."

I glared at him. I'd thought of something.

"I have a friend in the real world—we live together. Would Swords go after her?"

The King and the Knight exchanged a glance.

"Yes," they said in unison.

"Then, if I'm not going to be there to protect her, I need you to send someone to keep an eye on her and keep her safe."

"I can arrange that," said the Knight.

"Okay..." I cast about for anything else I should ask for. I couldn't think of anything. "Then I'll pretend to be a candidate. Just pretend. Until you find someone real to walk the Fool's Path."

The King stood with energy, his gold dressing gown rippling. He put out one hand to shake, saying: "Good. I like having something settled before breakfast. Or at breakfast. Makes the rest of the day seem less daunting." We clasped hands briefly and then he swept out of the room, carrying his coffee with him.

FIFTEEN

Sepulcher

I SETTLED BACK INTO MY chair.

"Is he always like that?" I asked.

"What do you mean?" asked the Knight.

"Like he's moving faster than everyone else. And doesn't quite care about anything."

The Knight didn't smile. "He cares about all of it. And no, he wasn't always like this."

I snorted and drank more coffee.

I could see a troubling thought in the Knight's face. He didn't have a great poker face. Or he pretended not to. Fucking Arcana, but this place was already bending my mind and making me paranoid. I decided to ask the King if I could do anything to speed up his search for candidates.

"What is it?" I asked the Knight, when it seemed like he wasn't going to speak despite the pained I-have-something-to-say face he was making.

"Your mother," he said. "I don't... She's still lying in state. If you'd like to pay..."

...my respects. I finished the sentence in my head and blinked. *It would be good to make sure she's really dead.* My thought made me ashamed, but that's what it was. I didn't say it out loud to the Knight.

"You said she was a good Queen," I said instead. "What makes you say that?"

He was flustered. "She was..." He shook his head. "Whatever I say won't be enough," he continued finally. "It would take forever to express it all, and individual-ly—I can say she was clever, that she protected her num-bered cards, that she was a strategist, that she saved my life and the King's a handful of times, that she was pow-erful and precise with her magic. Yet, what does it amount to, really? She was a good Queen. I'm sorry she wasn't a—" he changed directions mid-thought and finished with: "Why do you hate her?"

I'd been waiting for that one.

"She let my father die."

I'd rehearsed that line forever. Every time my family life came up in college, every time it came up with Delia. *Why do you hate your mother?* I'd had that answer on the tip of my tongue a hundred times and I'd always lied until now. "She may protect her cards, but she didn't protect him."

Even as I said it, I realized that it was like he'd said—it wasn't just that one thing, though that was what had pushed fear into hatred. It had been the breaking point, but she'd manipulated me all my life: taking away play-mates, controlling who I saw, what I learned, who I spoke to, forced me to be cruel, to learn to be hard early—it didn't fit into words, let alone into a minute or two of speech or a day or two of acquaintance.

"She was a terrible mother," I said, lamely.

The Knight turned away from me, but didn't have anything to say.

"I would like to see the body. For closure," I lied.

∞

The Knight of Wands took me to a pair of tall wooden doors, and left me there—saying that he had a few things to attend to, he would see me in the afternoon and if I needed to find my room again, any of the household servants would be able to take me there.

The doors were ornately carved with angels. I pushed them open, refusing to let the dread overcome me.

Beyond was a chapel—stone walls and stone floors all illuminated with small candles. The room wasn't large—it felt intimate, me and my mother's body.

They'd lain her out on a slab of stone, like Snow White in the fairy tale. The air of the chapel was cool, and once I was inside the room, the wooden doors closed on their own—by their own weight or by magic.

She looked older than I thought of her and peaceful in a way that seemed wrong. She was robed in soft orange and yellow with her hair—more golden than brown—arranged around her face. The flickering lights of the little candles made it almost seem like she was moving—sleeping instead of dead.

Wary of magic, I touched her wrist—just in case. She was cold, freezing and stiff to the touch.

There was a place for me to kneel beside her, and I did, wondering what I should do—or perhaps who I should pray to. Or if I should pray for her.

I knelt, staring at her face, waiting to feel more than I did.

I finally noticed the fine lines on her face—bloodless splits in her skin, like she'd been covered in paper cuts. I thought of the thin, thin slit on my arm where the air construct had cut me—thinner than paper, sharper than knives. They were all over her face and her hands.

The Knight had stopped when he tried to describe how she died.

My anger surprised me—the candles roared up around me in sudden fire—brightening the room and searing my eyes. I jumped up, sudden fear of myself quenching the anger and a handful of the candles.

I left the room.

The sooner I got out of the City the better.

SIXTEEN

Her Deck

Left to my own devices, I decided to explore the building I'd been given rooms in. It was strange to walk a baroque hallway and then stick my head into rooms that clearly belonged in other buildings and time periods. I took my time, getting my bearings and being nosy. No one told me off for poking into different rooms. I found my bedroom again and spent some time tracing routes to the front door of the building and to the breakfast room. Feeling somewhat better now that I knew the way out, I returned to my room—thinking vaguely of napping.

That, sadly, was driven from my mind when I noticed a black velvet bag and a note waiting on my bed. The note read:

Charity —

This was your mother's. I thought she would want you to have them.

— Knight of Wands

I appreciated that he didn't say that he thought I would want them. I'd begun to feel bad for the Knight somewhere along the line.

I wondered what he'd been called before 'Knight of Wands' and with slight horror realized that I didn't know what my mother's name had been before she was the Queen of Wands. Would anyone know? "Waits" was my father's name.

I sat staring at the Knight's signature and wondering about naming conventions in the City as a way to avoid examining the tokens my mother had left behind. He meant well. At least, I thought he did.

It was her tarot deck, of course, a living deck like mine. That would be the most important object she owned.

I took it up, and felt hostility from the cards. They were not interested in me. They wanted her and I was no substitute. Stubbornly, I opened the soft velvet bag and took them out. The edges were well worn, the backs painted in red and gold. On the top of the deck, guarding it, was Judgement. In the image a storm boiled in the sky, revealing and concealing trumpeting monsters and angels. Below, hands reached out of the ground, out of their graves.

I shuffled through the deck, looking at her cards.

Decks and cards in the City are made with a few different purposes. Some were built to be disposable—to be used on things like constructs. A person embodying a card—be they Major or Minor Arcana—could use their own card to imbue or animate something with their magic. Then there were decks like this one—a personal deck, often a living deck, that were used for other sorts of magics. Those magics were myriad. Everything from the Knight using the eight of wands to travel back to the City to the divinatory spread the King had been studying the night before. A well trained enchanter could use one card for a variety of purposes.

I dug into my suitcase, pulled out my box and from that my own deck. It looked bright and new next to my mother's. I shuffled through, trying to find my Judgement card.

Mine was different—of course, all living decks are. It showed clouds parting over a single feminine figure, the sunlight casting it in silhouette. No angels, but trumpets lined the edge of the card.

I considered the two cards, the darkness in my mother's deck and the hope in mine.

I shuffled through my deck and found her card—the queen of wands. Then, curious, I found the knight. He hadn't been the Knight when my deck was painted, but still—the face on my card was his. I tried to remember what my old knight card had shown before I left the City, but I couldn't. It had been a long, long time since I'd looked at my cards. For the sake of completing the set, I dug out the king and the princess of wands. My king card looked much like he had in my brief glimpse of his power—enthroned in his lion patterned robe. My princess was turned away, her face invisible in a cloud of black hair and bowed over her wand.

Going back to my mother's deck I searched for her wand court cards. The king here was much the same as mine, but slumped a little. Weary. The pose of the princess was similar as well—but instead of curly black hair, the face was hidden in straight brown hair. Like my hair. She wore a flowing orange tunic, her legs were covered in dark blue leggings. Like jeans.

I put that card away fast.

The knight card was different too—my knight of wands rode his horse, staring off into the distance. Hers knelt in supplication, his face turned up, his eyes closed—innocent and trusting and generous. Uncomfortable, I put him away too.

I couldn't find the queen of wands in my mother's deck. I went through her cards more slowly, and still didn't see it.

I put my deck away, and then began to order hers—setting aside the Major Arcana and ordering the Minor into their Suits. When I'd finished, I still had no queen of wands in my mother's deck.

I shuffled her deck back together, and tried to think through what it meant that she was missing from her own deck. She would have had the deck with her when she died. Would someone have taken it? What could a person do with the personal card from the living deck of a Court Card?

I'd begun to find the edges of my knowledge when it came to magic. I was going to need to push those edges out further. My out-of-date, teenaged perspective on the City itself wasn't going to be enough either.

As I finished putting the Queen's deck away, I heard voices in the hall. My stomach knew who it was before my mind did.

"In here?"

The door of my room opened without anyone knocking and Delia ran towards me. She threw her arms around me, squeezing me like it had been months and not less than twenty-four hours.

"Charity! Oh my god! I can't believe this!"

I hugged her back, eyes turned to my doorway where the bemused Knight of Wands stood holding Alphonso.

SEVENTEEN

Definitions of 'Safety'

"DELIA," I SAID, WHEN SHE let me go enough to breathe again. "What are you doing here? How did... What did he tell you?"

"He told me everything!" Delia looked around and amended: "Well, not everything. There hasn't been time. But he told me enough! I knew you weren't crazy, kitten! I just knew it!"

"What do you mean?"

"All the cards in the windows! All the weird superstitions! I knew it was something like this!"

"You knew that I came from a secret magical city ruled by tarot cards?"

"Yes! I mean, no! But I knew it was something like this. Can you set things on fire?" she asked.

"I..." Having trouble keeping up with Delia wasn't a new feeling for me, but this was more *Delia* than even I was used to. "How did you know that?" I asked.

"Ha! I knew it!" she pronounced. "I can't *believe* you didn't tell me." She tried and failed to keep the accusation and hurt out of her voice. She was angry I hadn't told her.

My gut clenched. "I didn't think you'd believe me," I said, honest and somewhat ashamed that the Knight had gotten to explain things instead of me.

"I guess it is rather unbelievable, but really, you should have told me. You could have set something on fire to prove it."

"I'm sorry," I said.

She hugged me again, squeezing like hell: "It's okay, kitten. I'm glad I know now."

"I'm glad you know too, but..." I scowled at the Knight of Wands. He was watching us, absently petting Alphonso. The cat seemed—to my annoyance—to approve of the Knight.

"May I have a word, Sir?" I asked, reverting to formal address.

"Of course," he said. He set the cat down and I disentangled myself from Delia—who went to poke around the closets like I had that morning. I stepped into the hallway and the Knight followed me.

"The *fuck* are you thinking?" I asked. "You said you would make arrangements to keep her safe." I took a soothing breath. I wasn't going to set anything on fire.

"I have," he said, surprised. "There's nowhere safer for her than here, in the heart of our palace."

"The City," I said, still holding onto my temper with all my might. "Is not safe. It is more dangerous than anywhere in the real world. There's magic here. How is this keeping her safe?"

He frowned at me. "In the mundane world, there are no rules," he said. "There is no way of saying 'she is ours, do not touch her' that Swords will acknowledge. We cannot complain to Swords for sending constructs after you—or her—out there. It's beyond our boundaries. Here in the City there are rules. There is etiquette and a way things are done. They won't touch her here, because the Court of Wands can come after them in any number of ways if they do—we can call on Justice or attack on our own or appeal to the other Courts. It's the safest place for her."

I let out a hissing breath, intending to reply, but with the breath came—surprising me—a tongue of flames. We were close enough together that he had to jump back to avoid my fiery breath singeing his eyebrows. I clapped my hands to my mouth, horrified.

He got over his shock and said, "You have got to at least train yourself not to spit fire—didn't anyone teach you it was rude?"

"I didn't mean to!" I said. "That's never happened before."

Then I realized he was laughing at me, looking down at me through sandy lashes.

"You do need to practice some control," he said. "While you're here anyway."

I was spared saying anything else by Delia.

"Kitten?" she called. "Why on earth are you wearing jeans when you could be wearing this?" She pushed open the door and stood there holding up a ridiculous cupcake of a dress.

I stared at her, mortified.

The Knight said, "I agree with you, Miss Delia.

Perhaps, as her friend, you can talk some fashion sense into her?" He meant it and not as a joke.

Delia smiled a dazzling smile up at him. "I can certainly try," she said and grabbed my arm, pulling me inside. "And then you can show me some of this City of yours!"

"I don't know if that's..."

"A good idea, if we're careful," said the Knight of Wands. "Charity hasn't had a chance to go out since she got here."

I glared at him while Delia shut the door.

She listened, waiting for his footsteps to recede and then she said, "Are all the Knights that pretty, or is it just yours?"

EIGHTEEN

Card Zero

DELIA WAS SERIOUS ABOUT GOING out to see the City and she continued cagey about how exactly the Knight of Wands had convinced her to come with him. I didn't push it. She really was annoyed with me for keeping the City a secret—and when she was ready I was sure we'd talk about it. I tried to give her the same space she'd given me when I was wrestling with the constructs and the Knight's appearance.

In the meantime, she took great delight in dressing us both in City garb. Delia wore one of the more elaborate costumes we'd found in my closet. Her skirt had several petticoats—all in shades of red—and the overskirt and dress was yellow. Delia looks good in most colors, including yellow. She'd even put on a tall wool hat—one covered with felted flowers and bright crimson humming-birds. A red jacket with white fur at the cuffs completed her ensemble.

She badgered me out of wearing jeans, but I still wore pants—in a shade of red so dark they were almost black—paired with a pale orange jacket with a high collar and a minimum of black embroidery at the neck and cuffs. My favorite thing we'd found for me were the shoes—fancy combat boots with brass buckles all the way up the sides to my calf.

Once we were ready, we sent Rosette to inform the King—I wasn't sure who to inform, to be honest, but Rosette didn't seem surprised when I said the King—that we wished to go out into the City and would require an escort.

Which is how we ended up beyond the walls of the Palace of Wands, on the winter streets of the City with four guards in the livery of Wands and the Seven of Wands to keep us safe. Delia was only slightly disappointed when it became apparent that the Knight would not be going with us.

The Seven was a huge man, with white blonde hair and warm brown skin. He'd tattooed his wands onto his arms—the ink a shining metallic gold. Despite the cold he wore an open sleeveless red vest, with an elaborate wand embroidered and beaded on the back. He was also the Captain of the Guard for Wands and, like me, he'd disliked the idea of Delia and I leaving the Palace. It was the King who had—to my surprise—convinced him.

"It's important not to seem afraid," was the King's argument for our little adventure.

"Even if we are?" I'd asked.

"Especially then."

The winter streets were full—the misting breath of

City denizens creating a fog around head height. In the daylight, I was surprised by how much color was packed into everything. The sky was grey, but under a layer of slush the streets were gold and white stone—and treacherously slick. The ornate frames around shop windows, the canopies on carriages and rickshaws over doorways, the clothing—all of it was gold and orange, deep purples, and so, so many shades of red.

We kept to the main street—a wide boulevard full of walking and riding traffic—but we passed innumerable tempting alleyways, each of which offered the flash of a strange sign, or a stone stairway, an odd door or sometimes a snatch of music. The sounds of footfalls, conversations, cart and carriage wheels were all muted by the winter air, and everything smelled cold.

Delia was fascinated, delightedly pointing out details to me all the way. "Did you see? Is that a monkey in that window? What will this look like in spring when those window boxes bloom? Is he on a unicycle?"

I was confused.

This wasn't the City I remembered: dangerous and cruel and poisoned from within. There were too many people laughing. There were children around, for the World's sake, running and sliding on the stone street, swinging around the filigreed iron lamp posts.

I wondered if this was the real reason the King had encouraged us to go out. So I could see a different side of the City.

I hadn't left the Palace of Wands much as a child. There wasn't a reason to. Now that I thought about it, one of the reasons I was nervous to go out and see the City was that my mother had always impressed on me how dangerous it was. Another bit of damage from her. It was looking like it was another lie as well.

"What is that?" asked Delia.

We'd come upon an intersection with another main street—to our right it continued much like the street we were on. To our left was an enormous Asian gate. It was orange, with curved blue ceramic roof tiles. It topped the height of the three story brownstones beside it. Hanging under the center of the gate was a rounded red lantern that was bigger than I was—like a paper lantern, but it couldn't have been paper, could it? The front was covered in black calligraphy.

"I don't know," I said. "I'm sure it's modeled on something in the real world."

"The Kaminarimon," said the Seven. "It belongs to Strength."

Neither Delia nor I knew what that was, but Delia asked the Seven: "Can we go that way?"

The Seven gave her a small bow and we went through the gate, under the red lantern. Beyond, the street was lined with shuttered stands—clearly a market of sorts. Although there were curtains over the stalls, people still packed densely in the street—and ahead of us was a second gate, like the one we'd already passed under—and a second red lantern.

As we approached the second gate, a wave went through the crowd—people stepping aside for someone. It was in the same way they did for us and our guards, but with a much wider space given to the person they were clearing the way for.

The person wore a loose shirt—black with enormous yellow flowers printed on it—and carried a large dirty gold handkerchief, folded into a bag and to carry something. One foot was bare in the slushy street, the other wore a pink plastic flipflop. Both were red with cold.

I froze, searching for a way for us to get further out of the way. It was no use. The person had seen us and came directly for us. The guards got out of their way, and they stopped in front of Delia, smiling sweetly. Innocently. Foolishly.

"Hello," they said. "Who are you?"

"I'm Delia," she said, before I could stop her. I'd put a hand on her arm hoping that if we cleared the way that the Fool would keep walking.

They didn't. They stood facing us head on.

"And you?" said the Fool to me. Curious, joyful.

"Charity, Arcana," I said, using the generic title of respect for one of the Major Arcana.

"Oh!" they clapped their hands with glee and the contents of the handkerchief jingled. "I waved to you! You knew me! How very nice to meet you properly? It is, right? I thought so once. I'm so pleased to share the road with you both."

My stomach dropped. I remembered the waving figure, sitting on the roof the night I arrived in the City. Last night.

"You are mistaken, Arcana," I said. "Neither of us is on the Fool's Path."

"Oh," said the Fool. "Oh. I thought you were. My mistake. I'm often mistaken."

They reached out and patted my face and then skipped

onwards into the City. I breathed a sigh of relief and found that Delia was laughing at me.

"What?"

"The way you talk here!" she said. " 'You are mistaken!'" she parroted me with an attempt at imitating the City's accent.

"Oh god, I don't still have the accent do I?" I asked. I hadn't noticed, but then I hadn't been paying attention.

"You do!" she laughed. "It's not all the time, but it sneaks out. Who was that? Why were you scared of her?"

"Scared of them," I corrected her. "That was the Fool—the first in the Major Arcana."

"Card number one," she said, more impressed.

"Card zero," I corrected again.

"Oh," she looked back to where the Fool had stopped to talk to a pigeon. "That's a little sad."

I'd never thought of it that way.

"Why were you scared of them?" asked Delia, taking my arm and pulling me through the second orange gate with its red lantern.

"Because that's who has to initiate you into training to become one of the Court Cards," I said. "And they aren't always... predictable about how they do things. I don't want us to get stuck here accidentally."

"Why not?" said Delia.

"Pardon?"

"You can't seriously be thinking of going back to American Fasteners instead of staying in an enchanted city."

"Well, I'm not going back to American Fasteners... but I..."

Delia's eyes were turned up to what appeared to be a temple. We walked inside, hushed and careful—watching for cues from the people of the City and our guards.

The ceilings were painted murals and there was an offertory box at the front of the main room where people bowed. A steady clink of coins falling into the box punctuated the gentle hum of people moving and speaking reverently. Behind the offertory—removed from the adherents to the card Strength—was a gold box, or perhaps a miniature golden house for the icon of the temple to inhabit. I wondered what was inside here and what was inside in the real world.

I'd forgotten why I wanted to go back to the real world at all. The serenity of the temple, the beauty of the City, the smile on Delia's face and even the friendliness of the Fool conspired to make me forget. I had to think about it.

Why did I want to go back?

Because it's dangerous, I imagined the words in my mother's voice and almost disregarded them—but it reminded me why I was here. My mother—the Queen of Wands—had been murdered in this City. As much as I disliked agreeing with her, I did.

The City was beautiful, more than I remembered, but it wasn't safe. Delia didn't know what she was getting into. I would have to try to explain it to her later—and talk about why, as magical as I'm sure it seemed to someone who didn't have any history here, we needed to get out as soon as we could.

NINETEEN

Face to Face

Aᴛᴇʀ ᴇxᴘʟᴏʀɪɴɢ ᴛʜᴇ ǫᴜɪᴇᴛ ᴛᴇᴍᴘʟᴇ, the noise and the bright winter sunshine outside startled me. I blinked and shaded my eyes. Beyond the gate and its enormous lantern, the empty market stalls had transformed while we were inside—all the shops were open and the merchants of the City were out in force. Street food vendors sold scoops of spiced insects, brightly colored candies and crisp shrimp grilled on sticks. A handful sold mugs of steaming cider and I could smell it from where we stood.

Glass baubles, small carvings and household items— from lanterns to wooden spatulas to umbrellas—were all for sale. I looked at the Seven to see if this worried him at all, but I caught a slight smile on his features for the first time.

Following his eyes, I found he was watching a merchant with a cage of cats on her back. She set down the cage between two stalls and pressed something on the side of it. It expanded and bent until it was a circular pen instead of a rectangular cage. The cats—entirely unfazed by this— explored the confines of the space with bored meows.

Delia was also delighted. She strolled in among the miniature shops, attracting compliments on her hat and calls from everyone to stop and see what she would see. Two of our guards followed her. The merchants tried to catch my eye as well, but I kept moving, pretending that I didn't hear them and watching the crowd, with what I thought was an unreasonable feel of trepidation—

I saw them right as the Seven's broad hand came down on my shoulder. Three Swords were coming towards us, and one—one I already knew. The Knight of Swords' card had been in every single one of the constructs sent after me. He looked exactly like his card. At first I welcomed the little heat in my hands that told me I could burn something—and then I remembered the garden. There were a lot of people here—and they didn't have the magical protection against fire that the House of Wands overflowed with.

The Seven stayed near me—another two guards behind him.

The Knight had seen us, of course. He might have come to the market just to see us.

He wore the grey and pale blue of Swords— a long coat that almost brushed the street—belted in silver with his sword hanging from his hip. His face was narrow, cheekbones pointed, and his hair pulled back into a perfectly straight ponytail.

Delia didn't know what was going on, but she knew

it wasn't good. She looked from the Knight—approaching along the market street—to me and the Seven—waiting for him. For the moment, she stayed where she was. Thankfully.

The Knight didn't pretend to have business with anyone else. He walked straight to me. The Seven didn't exactly stand between us, just one step in front of me and slightly to the left.

The Knight of Swords glanced at the Seven, dismissed him with his eyes and focused on me.

I'd never had to face someone who'd tried to kill me before. It was new. Unsettling. He was—after all—just another card, another Court Card. I remembered trying to breathe with the air construct around me, suffocating me. He'd done that.

I should have been afraid. Aside from anything else, that would have been more convenient. Instead, I was angry.

Fucking great.

The Knight of Swords bowed to me. No one but our own parties were looking at us, but everyone was watching. I bowed back. I didn't try to curtsy.

"It's a pleasure to meet you in person, Miss Waits," said the Knight. He wasn't either particularly short or tall—but his voice was deep, almost a bass.

"It's a pleasure to meet you too," I said. "Are you trying to kill me today?"

He pretended surprise and offense. "Not here, Miss Waits, I assure you," he said. "I would never be so rude."

"Rude?" I asked. "I suppose that's one description for assassins."

"Assassins..." he repeated. "No, I wouldn't call those trifles 'assassins'. If I'd sent assassins they would have been of a much higher quality. Really, Miss Waits, it was a compliment."

My magic must have been on a harder boil than even I knew. A few people near us were edging away—and I'm sure that whatever the faults of the Knight of Swords, a lack of control certainly wasn't one. Delia was silently negotiating with her guards. She wanted to come closer to me. They wanted her to stay where she was—and out of the Knight of Swords' sight. I was careful not to look directly at them.

"I see..." said the Knight. I didn't know what he saw, but I didn't particular like it, or care. "Well... that's interesting."

"What exactly?"

"I admit," he said. "I didn't put much store in your mother's plan to send you away. It left you vulnerable. And ignorant. It didn't take much to find you. It did make you powerful. It's fascinating. You're like a leopard that's convinced she's a housecat."

My mother's plan to send me away. Is that what she told the City? Is that what actually happened? Was all of this her plan all along?

I didn't say anything. I was entirely focused on not setting the market on fire. Delia helped. It was easier to pretend I was in the real world with her there—I had a lot of practice putting off my firestorms in the real world and saving them for a more appropriate moment.

"I hope you'll forgive me," said the Knight. "Let me welcome you to the City. It's better that you're here."

"Why?"

"It makes things more... even. I don't like winning by default. That's not how we do things in Swords. Your mother, now, she liked to win in any way she could. " The venom in his voice surprised me. He'd hated my mother.

"She was a bit of a bitch," I said, without thinking.

The Seven stiffened and the Knight of Swords looked shocked.

I smiled. I was angry, but he'd missed his mark by trying to provoke me using my mother.

"I'm not in the habit of forgiving people who try to kill me," I said, leaning into the silkiness of my City accent. "But as you pointed out, my time away from the City has given me rather a rough manner and perhaps left me ignorant. Shall we start again, Sir?" On impulse, I offered him my hand.

He took it, flipped it so my palm faced down and kissed the back of my hand. His lips were dry—like paper.

I tried not to show my surprise and pulled back, but he held onto my hand hard.

"Well met then, Miss Waits. I give you my word, you'll know when I'm really interested in killing you. Briefly, anyway." He let go of me and bowed. "Best of luck on the Fool's Path, Charity Waits." He turned, walking away from the Seven and I with his minions drifting behind him—without a glance at Delia.

"That could have gone better," said the Seven.

"Time to get back to the palace?" I said.

"Yes, ma'am."

TWENTY

The Dead Past

ONCE WE WERE OUT OF the impromptu market outside the temple, Delia had a few questions for the Seven and I: "What was that? Who was that? Did he really try to kill you?"

I answered: "That was a test, he was the Knight of Swords and yes, he definitely did."

"Oh," said Delia. "I like our Knight better."

"*Your* Knight?" said the Seven, wonderingly.

"The Knight of Wands," said Delia.

The Seven chuckled.

We walked back to the Palace of Wands. Delia was not pleased to cut short our visit to the City and so we compromised and decided to return home on foot instead of taking a rickshaw back to safety. The Seven said it looked better to walk. I didn't particularly care what it looked like, but I didn't want to fight with Delia. I didn't want to scare her either.

"So..." Delia said. "Why exactly is the Knight of Swords trying to kill you, chérie?"

"We—the Court of Wands—are nearly at war with the Court of Swords."

"Nearly?"

The Seven shrugged. "Not official yet..." he said and hefted his wand, his focus. It was more of a quarterstaff than a wand—polished wood, banded in gold and shod in iron.

"And why are we,"—I flinched at the pronoun Delia chose—"at war with the Court of Swords?"

"Because *they're* always at war with the Court of Swords," I said. "The Courts are always fighting for power in the City. Everyone hates everyone and everyone has a grudge or an axe to grind or something. It's all blood feuds that no one can remember the origin of anymore."

The Seven, who hadn't been particularly jolly before, was now downright annoyed.

"The current tension," he said. "Stems from a series of brutal and retaliatory murders—the Princess of Wands and now the Queen."—He didn't look at me.—"There have been attempts on the lives of the King and the Knight as well. Swords are coming for us, and they will not be inclined to deal kindly with any of those loyal to the Court of Wands should they manage to destroy the Court and the Suit entirely."

Delia raised a remonstrating eyebrow at me and turned to ask questions of the Seven, clearly finding my interpretation lacking.

"So, why was the Princess of Wands killed?" she asked. "What were the circumstances?"

The Seven hesitated, uncomfortable, but said, "It was done—we believe—partially in retaliation for the death of the Princess of Swords some years before. That was an unfortunate incident. The Queen of Wands was driven to grief by her lover's death and... things got out of hand."

Delia glanced at me, recognizing the entrance of my father into the story. She patted my arm.

"They weren't together then," I said, and then bit my lip. There was more I could say about it—she'd chosen to kill the Princess of Swords instead of rescue my father. At the moment though, I didn't want undermine Wands without knowing what the consequences might be. I would want to get my facts very straight before I did that at all.

"So the Queen of Wands kills the Princess of Swords and then the... who killed the Princess of Wands?"

"It was in a duel with the new Knight of Swords."

"There are duels?" asked Delia. "How does that work?"

"They're usually fought with magic," said the Seven, "though on that occasion it was with steel and magic."

"Hmmm..." said Delia, and then to me, "I begin to see what you mean about the City being dangerous. If you can be challenged to magical duels."

The Seven smiled. "No one will challenge you to a duel, Miss Delia. It's rare outside of the Suits—the Court and numbered cards—and certainly not something anyone would do to an entirely untrained young lady from the mundane world. Even Swords would not be so dishonorable."

"Untrained..." said Delia. Then she perked up. "Do you mean that *I* could learn magic?"

"Oh," said the Seven. "I don't know. It's rare to find a

strong sorcerer in the mundane world. You could still be tested and see—most people can learn at least a cantrip or two, I've heard. I've never met anyone who came to the City from the mundane world before. So I'm not certain."

Delia appeared ready to burst from excitement. When my smile did not adequately match her enthusiasm she grabbed my arms and spun me around on the street—her petticoats flaring out.

"I'm so glad you're not crazy!" she said. "I'm so glad I'm not crazy! I might learn some magic!"

"I'm glad we're not crazy too," I said, laughing.

TWENTY-ONE

Trust and Truce

THAT NIGHT DELIA AND I decided to take dinner in my room. It had been a long day and even Delia was ready to relax and avoid new people for a bit. She did, however, opt to continue wearing her enormous cupcake of a dress.

Alphonso took a good deal of joy in batting at the ribbons on Delia's poofy sleeves and skirts. The cat seemed to be settling in as well as Delia.

"What made you think I could set things on fire?" I asked.

"Oh, you know," said Delia. "There were a few signs, and I rather suspected that there was something *actually* arcane about you, honey. Ever since that one boy—what was his name?"

"James," I said, flinching.

"You made his cigarette do that 'burst into flames' thing, didn't you?"

102

"I did," I admitted. "He was being an ass to you. You deserve better."

Delia threw back her head and laughed. "He was very pretty. That's about the best that can be said."

"Less pretty with soot on his face. And that expression."

"Decidedly," said Delia. "Anyway—after that I started paying attention. I nearly caught you lighting the fireplace, I think."

I nodded. I remembered that too.

"I'm sorry," I said.

"For what, chérie?"

I took in a deep breath and tried to get it all out: "For not telling you about all this. I never thought I would be back and I told myself it didn't matter, but it did and I was wrong. I was afraid you'd think I was nuts. Or that I'm dangerous. Which I am. You're in danger now. Like really. And it's my fault. I'm really, *really*, sorry."

Delia stared down at her hands, folded in the lap of her extravagant yellow gown.

She thought in silence for a small eternity, then said: "I accept."

"Oh, Dee," I said. It wasn't that simple. It couldn't be.

"Is there anything else I should know now?" she asked, serious.

"I don't know," I said, wracking my brain. "I mean, there's a lot—about the courts and the City and my deal with the King..."

"You know what I meant," said Delia. "You're not like, a werewolf or anything?"

"Oh," I thought about it. "No. Nothing as crazy as this. I don't think so."

"Good! Then let's eat and you can start explaining everything."

∞

We ate and talked. While I was showing her my tarot deck, we were interrupted by a knock on the door.

"Come in," I said, and I recognized the blonde servant—Rosette—from earlier when she entered. "What is it?" I asked.

"The King of Wands would like a word with you, Miss Waits, if you would wait upon him?"

"Of course," I said, even though I didn't mean it. I glanced an apology to Delia. "Now?"

"If it please you."

I sighed. "I'm sorry. I should probably go."

Delia waved me on. "Oh do, and then you can tell me all about him when you come back."

So I stood and followed Rosette.

"Did His Majesty say what he wanted?" I asked.

"No, Miss," said the servant.

We walked on, through the twisting corridors. The building was a bit like a palace, really. We didn't go back to the garden, but rather to what appeared to be the King's private apartments. Guards in gold and orange stood outside the room, and the servant brought me in through an ornate door highlighted in gold leaf.

"Miss Waits," she announced me.

The room was spare by the standards I'd seen of the City. A wooden desk and thick hangings over the windows, bookshelves and a small work table with a chest of tiny drawers over it.

The King stood by his desk, staring off into space. He glanced at me as I came in, blinked and then nodded.

"Thank you," he said and Rosette retreated, leaving us alone.

"Did you enjoy the City, Miss Waits?" he asked.

"I suppose," I said.

"Good, good," he said. He seemed to search for another topic, and then to give up. "I am told that you met the Knight of Swords."

"Yes..."

"And that he insinuated an assurance that you will be walking the Fool's Path."

"Yes."

"Good, good," he said again.

"Majesty?"

"Yes?"

"What did you want?" I asked, hoping he'd get to the point.

"I wanted to make a decision about whether or not to host your presentation soon. A public display of our support for you. A sort of party," he explained. "It's not a decision really. We need to. We need to soon. I don't like it. It feels like we've been boxed into something with this... it's all too... easy? No, not easy. It's neat. I don't like it—and I don't think you're ready for it."

"What do you mean 'I'm not ready for it'?"

"You incinerated half my garden last night," said the King.

"Ah," I said.

"If we admit that you're *that* untrained—so untrained we can't show you in public..."

He let his fingers rap on the desk.

"You did show me in public today," I pointed out. "I didn't blow anything up."

"You were close," he said. "Seven said you were clearly near a breaking point—to the point where any child could have seen your aura."

"Ah," I said again.

"However," he said. "That might work to our advantage. Show you as a loose cannon."

He shook his head. "I'll have to think about it. What I wanted to inform you of was that we will be holding a celebration—in your honor—in a few days. Your formal presentation to the Fool. Ten is working out the details."

"Oh," I said. Terribly articulate, me.

He raised an eyebrow. "No temper tantrum?"

"I'm sorry about that," I said. I took a breath. Apparently it was an evening for apologies. Better get them all out of the way at once. "I... How well did you know my mother?"

The King frowned. "Quite well."

"I've been thinking about... a few things, with regards to her. Among other things... she..." I wasn't sure how to say this. "Majesty, she taught me to hate the City. I thought it was an accident, but I don't know if it was. She taught me... she taught me to distrust you. All Court Cards. And everybody else too."

"That sounds like her," he said. "She always wanted... control and did not trust easily. If she did at all. I'm trying to pick up the threads of a number of things she'd set in motion that I don't understand yet. Which she never told me about."

"I thought I'd separated her ideas from my own," I said. "I thought that realizing she was a monster meant that I'd broken free. Now I'm... I'm worried she had another plan I can't see. I'm worried she wanted me to distrust you. I know I can't trust you, but also that maybe that's her in my head talking... Maybe she even wanted me to hate her."

The King smiled slightly. "You overthink things, Miss Waits."

"Yes," I said.

"I think even your mother was not as complicated as you are making her," he said. "You give her credit for all her intentions manifesting in the way she intended them. That isn't true for anyone."

I nodded. He was right. Even dead she was still giving me headaches.

"Do you know who killed her? Exactly?" I asked.

The King shook his head.

"The Knight of Swords hated her," I said.

"Yes," the King agreed. I thought about that and finally decided on something.

"After... after I'm settled in. I'd like to help find out. Who killed her and why," I said. I surprised myself, finding how true it was. I'd spent a long time practicing not caring about her.

"Certainly," said the King.

"Good," I said, echoing him. "Is that everything?"

"For now," he said, and then: "Miss Waits... the Knight of Wands. You may not want to talk to him about you mother that way. He was..."

"He was in love with her?" I guessed.

"Yes," said the King. "Very much so."

It made me sad, to think so. He seemed nice. Whether it was complicated or simple, my mother certainly was never nice. I would have to warn Delia.

"I'm sorry for him," I said.

"So was I," said the King and we left it at that.

TWENTY-TWO

My Presentation

THE NEXT FIVE DAYS WERE a blur. I got lessons on what the etiquette for this party would be. I was measured for clothing. I tried to learn how to dance and tried to relearn my City accent—so I'd sound less *parochial*. I practiced with fire magic, trying to summon it while I was not angry. No success there, partially because trying was frustrating as hell and made me angry—thus defeating the purpose of the exercise. I was getting better at *not* setting things on fire when I was angry though.

I tried not to be nervous. I tried not to think about the impending party. I reminded myself over and over again that it was all for show.

It didn't feel like show, though, and the clothing that arrived at my room the morning of the party didn't fucking help.

Much to my chagrin and Delia's joy, I was not allowed to choose what I wore to the celebration in *my honor*.

I'd have made some different choices, if I'd been consulted.

My costume evoked the Fool's traditional regalia. The sleeves were large and belled, the bodice tight and all of it very yellow. The short stiff skirt stuck out in a cone from my waist. It came almost down to my knees. Delia said that it reminded her a bit of a figure skating outfit, but with much nicer fabrics. I thought it looked a bit like a mushroom. My tarot deck sat at the left side of my waist, the case built into my dress at an angle for an easy draw.

I did put up a fight when it came to the shoes. I got to wear my boots with the buckles up the side.

Once I was in the dress, I had to sit while my hair was brushed and arranged with gold pins. A chipper young man did my makeup.

By the end, I looked like a stranger. Not horrible, just not at all like myself.

Delia—on the other hand—was allowed to have an opinion on her own costume and looked stunning in a floaty gown of orange and gold organza. Despite what I considered a dangerously full fluttering skirt she didn't step on the hem—even the very first time she went swishing around the room.

She, at least, was having a fantastic time. I tried not to spoil it for her, but that left me to worry on my own about my penchant for setting things on fire, about Delia's first social event in the City, and about the Court of Swords. I was definitely worried about the Court of Swords. Because they'd been invited to my party. It was traditional—apparently—that we invite *all the Courts* to my formal presentation to the Fool.

The King assured me that he did not expect anything from the Court of Swords but a cold rejection of the invitation, if that.

Somehow I didn't feel better.

Evening came fast. Before I knew it, I was standing in my fancy dress on a balcony, peering down at crashing ocean waves, surrounded by a few allies, a lot of strangers, and exactly one friend. Alphonso wasn't invited or I might have counted him, just to feel less lonely.

The sun was setting into the ocean—an ocean that had no other shores beyond this one. Behind me, it turned the glass in the City to orange and magenta and bright purple. We were up on a cliff—below those buildings and above the sea—and I wasn't sure what to call the structure itself. Which isn't entirely surprising, since it belonged to the Fool.

Palaces for the different Suits of the tarot were each in their own consolidated areas, but the Major Arcana had strongholds throughout the City too—single buildings or parks or palaces dedicated to them.

This place belonged to the Fool and was something between an ancient grecian temple, a cave, and a ballroom.

Three sides were open to the elements—the roof was made of white stone, curving into small arches, punctuated by circular murals, and held up by massive columns over a polished black marble floor. I could see my distorted reflection in the floor. Below where I stood on the balcony, stairways wound away from each other and back together towards the edge of the cliff. The rails undulated, their sides covered in rainbow mosaics. A fountain in the shape of an iguana—also covered in chips of blue and sea green glass—crouched between those stairs, staring out at the waves too. Colorful lanterns hung between the pillars around me and some spell kept the place warm without the use of fire—which might be seen as threatening at an event held by the Court of Wands.

Up here guests either clustered in small conversational groups with drinks in hand or danced between the pillars back by the only real wall. The dancers appeared and disappeared between the pillars, like a dream sequence in a movie—vibrant and moving in time with each other. The musicians—a fiddle, drums, and an upright bass—were hidden from my sight and their music reverberated strangely through the space—haunting echoes coming back to me at odd moments. The musicians were dressed in yellow, permanent devotees of the Fool, along with the servants who circulated with drinks and whimsical canapés—fruit cut into the shape of flowers and miniature pastry bindles.

I was drinking cranberry juice and water while hiding. Alcohol would have made the evening easier, but more dangerous too.

The number of introductions I'd endured in the last hour were enough to make a bloody extrovert need a moment alone. I'd met representatives from two of the other Courts: the King of Cups and the Knight and Princess of Disks, along with several of their numbered cards.

In Wands and Swords, the King is primarily a magician—the sorcerer charged with caring for their respective Aces. The Queens, then, are the political heads of the Court. In Cups and Disks, those roles are switched. I had to remind myself, therefore, that the King of Cups was a political entity more than a magical one. He wore a formal tunic that shimmered like the water below us and wore elaborate makeup, his face painted like a mask in white, green, and blue. I thought he was intimidating as hell.

The Knight and Princess of Disks were both pleasant, their manner dangerously disarming. They wore robes of moss green velvet and hundreds of precious stones. I think they ended up unimpressed with me, but not hostile.

Meanwhile, Delia was having the time of her life. She sipped champagne and pretended to be a dozen different sorts of things in the real world. She explained with a perfectly straight face to different guests that she was a fishmonger, a pop star's publicist or an archeologist. I had to stop listening so that my laughter wouldn't give her away. The Knight of Wands had caught on too, and was listening with his back to her, his shoulders shaking occasionally with concealed merriment while he talked to our Seven.

The King of Wands was deep in conversation with the King of Cups across the balcony—and comparing them I found myself thinking—in Delia's voice—that I preferred *our* King.

The Ten of Wands meanwhile, stood aloof and alone. Something seemed to be bothering her. She'd hardly spoken to me when I thanked her for putting this together. I supposed she didn't like me—not surprising given what I'd done to the King's garden.

In search of a moment alone, I'd found this place by the railing overlooking the ocean.

That's where the Fool found me.

TWENTY-THREE

The Fool's Advice

I DIDN'T SEE THE FOOL arrive at the party, but suddenly they were next to me, staring out at the sunset too. They wore a fantastic rainbow coat and no shoes at all. Their messy hair ruffled in the breeze and their eyes were brown and glittered with the dying light.

"Hello, Charity," said the Fool. "Welcome!"

After a quick double take and a nervous swallow, I said, "Hello, Arcana. Thank you."

The Fool seemed sad. "You're afraid of me?" they asked. Confused.

"No, Arcana," I said and then winced. "Maybe a bit."

"Why?" the Fool's voice was petulant.

"Because you're a Major Arcana. The first Major Arcana."

The Fool shook their head. "The zero-eth," they said with a smile. "Not the first."

I nodded. *That's sad,* Delia had said.

"And... that's not why you are afraid of me," continued the Fool. They playfully prodded my arm. "Why?" they asked. "What is it?"

I looked at the Fool. It was strange to see the oldness of an Arcana mixed in with the childish caprice of the Fool's position and their magic. Hard to remember they were monstrously powerful in the City and especially here—in a space dedicated to them.

I didn't know what to say, how to say that this was all for show and I wasn't really a candidate for the Fool's Path and I shouldn't be *presented* to them. I didn't want to be. Did I? The Fool caught something in my face and, voice abruptly too serious and too wise, they said, "It's always a choice, Charity."

"I don't..." I started to say, and then stopped. I'd been thinking, hard, about the City for the last few days, but I'd avoided admitting it to myself—easy with everything going on. Admitting aloud to an Arcana, to the Fool them-self, that I was tempted—that a part of me wanted the magic and maybe not as small a part as I'd thought—would be dangerous. That would be its own irrevocable choice—to even admit it aloud.

The Fool hummed sympathetically and they put a hand on my arm.

"It's okay. You're doing fine. You'll figure it out."

The gentleness of the gesture and the damned incipient kindness of the words had me tearing up. I was tired and I didn't think I was doing fine and worse, I still wasn't sure what I *wanted* to do.

I was saved from my emotions and dangerous intro-

spection by a sudden silence behind us, followed immediately by a wave of whispers.

I turned around with the Fool and we were both able
to catch the arrival of the representatives of the Court of
Swords: Ten figures in sky blue livery, with flashing silver
crests and literal swords.

I picked out the Knight of Swords quickly, elegant with
his slicked back white blonde ponytail. With him, wearing a fine silver crown, was a tall black woman. She had
a rapier at her hip and I couldn't tell what card she was—
but I would have bet she was the Princess of Swords. The
rest were guards. It was more protection than Disks or
Cups brought together—and there were no civilian lack-
eys with them. No attendants beyond their guards.

The Knight of Swords met my eyes. He made a bow
from across the black stone floor and commented to the
woman, gesturing towards myself and the Fool. She
turned an assessing eye on me, and I got to try to decide
who frightened me more—the Knight of Swords or her.
Too close to call.

The Fool clapped their hands together. "Everyone's
arrived!" they said.

They turned to me and took my hands. I felt weirdly
exposed, taking my eyes off the Swords.

"Listen to me," they said, fast and low, like we were
about to be separated forever, "sometimes our eyes
deceive us."

"What?" I asked.

"Sometimes," said the Fool. "A sandwich makes
everything better."

Their eyes drifted away from me, their attention caught

by a servant and their tray of canapés. The Fool let me go and left me.

Alone again, the atmosphere of the party—the temperature, the music, and the timbre of the conversation—all seemed more sinister with the arrival of the Swords.

The dense rows of columns meant that with every step my sight lines changed. I walked slowly, guests appearing and disappearing like I was at the center of a kaleidoscope, searching for the Swords. Instead, I found the King of Wands approaching me.

"Charity?"

He had spent more time on his appearance than usual. He still wore his black turtleneck, and his hair remained a mess of curls—but he'd added a long vest, made of cloth of gold. His boots, belt, and the holsters that held his deck and his focus all had filigreed gold work on them.

He wasn't exactly regal, but he wasn't unregal either. I wished I knew how to pull off something like that. Then they might not have asked me to wear the mushroom dress I had on.

"How did that go?" asked the King. He must have seen me with the Fool.

"Marvelously," I said, throwing on a smile—the way Delia would have.

He looked at me oddly. "Don't do that."

"Smile?"

"*Try* to smile," he corrected. "It's unsettling."

I gave up and rubbed my jaw—I'd forgotten about the makeup, and my fingers slid over the powder and grease on my face. I frowned at my fingertips, nonplussed, and the King closed his eyes for a moment—as though begging for patience.

"Come," said the King of Wands, and he put out a hand to me. "Time to dance. Are you ready?"

"Not really..."

"It can't be helped now."

TWENTY-FOUR

In Which I Dance

"WHY ARE THERE SWORDS HERE?" I asked as the King and I walked closer to the musicians.

"I don't know."

"You said they wouldn't come," I pointed out.

"I was wrong," he said without a smile. He seemed worried about it, so I stopped asking questions and hoped that he had a few contingency plans in place. Then I checked the exits—to leave one had to go outside the pillars and up a few flights of stairs to the City proper. Our other option was to jump in the ocean. In winter. It wasn't exactly the most convenient set up for an escape.

Besides sorting out my clothing and this venue and getting blitz lessons on etiquette and the different people who might attend our little soiree, I'd been given a few lessons in dancing. I wasn't nearly good enough to be comfortable.

"Relax," the King said, "Follow, and you'll be fine."

"I'm shit at both those things," I said.

"I know," he said. "Practice, practice, practice."

The King pulled me along. This close he smelled faintly of fire and iron, and I could see flecks of gold in his brown eyes. He was a good dance partner, and a good height for me too. I think I might even have been momentarily graceful myself. We passed in and out of sight of the other dancers, the musicians and the guests. I glimpsed Delia, proud and pretty next to a wryly smiling Knight of Wands. Next I got a chilling view of the Princess of Swords watching, her face impassive, arrogant and remote. Then I caught another odd expression from the Ten—she watched us with narrowed eyes. The King spun us carefully between the pillars, and despite everything, I found I was smiling.

"This is more pleasant than I thought it would be," I admitted.

"Dancing?"

"Yes," I said, though that was only part of it. I'd meant the party too. And the City. I'd meant all of it.

We spun past more guests. I caught a fleeting sight of the Fool's rainbow coat.

"This is significant, isn't it? Us dancing together. Traditional or something."

"Yes," said the King. He didn't try anything fancy— thank the World—but he was showing me off.

After another few steps, I asked: "What happens? If you can't find someone for the Path? What happens to Wands if Swords wins? Surely, there's always a House of Wands. They can't really destroy us. You."

"All Houses rise to prominence and fall. Sometimes to their utter destruction. Sometimes not. There have been times—decades—in the City where a Suit has been obliterated and their House disbanded. They do come back. So far."

I thought of his gardens and the palace itself. I thought of Rosette and all the people I'd taken lessons from in the last few days.

"You talk about it very calmly," I said.

I caught a glimpse of the weariness in him. He was on the brink of exhaustion, even now, dancing with me.

"The Wheel of Fortune turns," he said, referring to the tenth card of the Major Arcana. "It will be as it will be."

"Do you think that Wands is doomed?"

"No. Though going by the signs our position is... poor," he said.

"It would be strengthened by having someone on the Path?"

"It would."

"There must be tons of people who'd like to be a member of the Court. I thought..." I'd been thinking about the last time I was in the City, when someone else had walked the Path, and realized that—of course—it had been the King walking. He must have been very young, doing that. "Do I remember there being lots of candidates—trials even—before you walked the Path?"

"You do," he said.

"So what's changed? Where are all the candidates?"

"There are none."

"What?"

"It requires a great deal of raw strength—and to put

someone without real aptitude on the Path would be irresponsible."

"That's not what I asked."

"Lately," the King said, "anyone with the strength to walk is older—which is it's own problem. We don't know why."

I looked at him. "You don't know?"

The King managed a shrug while we were dancing. He stared over my shoulder and said, "The Wheel turns. Sometimes suits fall."

I turned my eyes out to the crowd too and thought about what it would mean for Wands to fall. The Seven wore another open vest embroidered in gold and he was laughing with a small woman wearing the rich velvety green of Disks. The Knight of Wands was trying to show Delia how to dance. She was giggling through the lesson and he was clearly torn between exasperation and being charmed. I couldn't help but smiling a little at those two. There was even something endearing about the standoffish Ten.

There's always a choice.

Are you really going to go back?

I asked the next questions fast: "Did you mean it? When you said I could play the part while you found someone else to be on the Path?"

"It's always a choice," said the King, echoing the Fool.

"You actually think I could do it? Survive the Fool's Path? Why? Because, I'm her daughter?"

He gave me a look. "Charity. Don't make me say something sentimental."

"What?" I asked. When he still seemed exasperated, I

said. "I actually don't know what you mean."

He said, "You ought to know that being her daughter doesn't matter. You could do it. Because of what you are. Not what she was."

I felt suddenly light in more than one way.

"Oh."

I don't know about you, but I don't actually make decisions all at once—and this one had crept up slowly, crowding me in from a dozen different directions while I carefully ignored it. The decision to try walking the Fool's Path came from Delia's delight in magic and from Seven's expression when he reminded me that the House of Wands was more than its Court. From that temple with the red lantern and the merchants outside it and from the Fool's stupid pink flipflop and their sweet smile. And from wanting the power to beat the shit out of the Knight of Swords—or the Princess—if I needed to.

"How do I do it?" I asked.

The King raised an eyebrow. "Why, Charity Waits, what on earth are you talking about?"

"You fucking knew I would end up doing it," I said, voicing a guess. "So don't pretend to be surprised." I paused. "How did you know?"

"You do know what they use our cards for in your real world, right?"

I remembered the spread of cards he'd been examining when I first arrived.

"World damn it," I said, "And you."

The King smiled. "Once you've chosen the Path it will come to you. You'll know when you're on it." He didn't make any further comment on my decision, but I thought he might be somewhat relieved. Maybe I was imagining it.

"Right," I said. "Of course that's how it'll work."

TWENTY-FIVE

The Knight's Grudge

THE SONG ENDED AND THE King of Wands bowed to me. I curtsied. That had been part of the lessons.

"As you said," the King commented. "That dance was a tradition and necessary for appearances. Would you like to continue dancing?"

More and more guests had given up their canapés in favor of swishing in time around the musicians, but before I answered the Knight of Swords approached us.

The King still held my hand, and I could feel him tense briefly at the sight of the enemy Knight. I never would have been able to tell if we hadn't been touching.

"Majesty," the Knight said to my King who nodded and said, "Sir."

He turned to me, icy cold and scornful, "Miss Waits. You're a very poor dancer. But determined."

"You are too kind, sir," I said, rolling my eyes.

The Knight sneered and made a show of taking in our clothes and then the general party. From the corner of my eye, I saw the Knight of Wands. He'd stopped talking to Delia and moved closer to us, paying close attention to the King, the Knight of Swords, and I.

"This celebration seems rather sudden, perhaps presumptuous?" said the Knight of Swords, "Since you returned to the City so recently, Miss Waits. Are you feeling fully prepared to walk the Path?"

"She knows that no one is truly prepared for the Path," said the King.

"Yet outstanding arrogance does run in her family. I can't imagine the Queen of Wands ever thinking she wasn't ready for... well, anything."

"Surely we can avoid speaking ill of the dead," said the King, disdainful in his turn.

"Dead?" said the Knight of Swords. "Ah, yes. You've been saying that."

I felt something strange then—like a sudden heat, except not actually warmth. It was magic. The King and the Knight of Wands nearby were both paying close attention to the Knight of Swords and were pulling in their own magic. They were getting ready for something. I glanced around, searching for Delia—she was standing with the Seven further away, both of them turned in our direction.

Between different pillars I caught sight of the Princess of Swords. The delegations from Disks and Cups were abruptly nowhere to be seen. I didn't see the Fool. They were probably somewhere behind me—I didn't want to look around to be sure.

What is going on?

I was agitated myself, annoyed enough to summon fire if I needed it.

The silence stretched awkwardly from the Knight of Sword's last comment.

I said, trying to understand: "You think we're lying about my—about the Queen of Wands' death?"

It felt like everyone held their breath.

The Knight of Swords laughed without mirth.

"I know it," he said. Something was very wrong. The Knight of Swords smiled at us. "Would you like me to prove it, Majesty?"

With an expression of pure venom he drew a card.

Everything that happened next happened very, very fast.

The King tried to come between the Knight and I, putting out a hand, fire spilling from his fingers, and his other hand reaching for his deck. The Princess of Swords sent a spell spinning towards the King of Wands—for a second I saw a card in her hand and there was something odd and shimmery about it. Her spell hit the King, distracting him. Delia shouted and the Seven grabbed her arm to keep her from coming towards me—while the Knight of Wands did charge forward, but from too far away. I reached for my own magic. The Knight of Swords was faster.

I glimpsed the card the Knight held towards me before his spell took effect. He held his three of swords—it showed a man in armor, holding a woman with three swords stuck in her breast, through her heart. A second later, I felt those swords.

I screamed and curled inwards, the sudden pain driving all the anger out of me. I fell down, feeling like my ribcage was split, pried apart like window shutters breaking free from my sternum.

My sight swam and tears ran down my face while I screamed.

Flashes of light burst in my vision and I didn't know if it was fire magic or pain.

I thought I was dead. I wished I was.

Someone was holding me. I thought it was Delia, but I could hear her shouting for me from further away.

I peeled my eyes open, and stared at the ceiling above me—a green and gold and blue mosaic, blurry through my tears. I turned my head slightly, and met the Fool's eyes.

"I don't understand," I whispered, hiccuping with the pain.

"Me neither," said the Fool, and they leaned down to plant a chaste kiss on my lips.

The Fool's magic is beginnings. It is optimism—misplaced or not—and reprieve and freedom from old debts. It is the place from which anything is possible.

When their lips touched mine, I suddenly saw the room as though looking down from that glittering glass studded ceiling.

The two Knights dueled across the room, wand to sword—sending sparks and gusts of magic up around them. It was hard to tell who was getting the better of that battle.

The King of Wands was lost in a surge of fire and magic. Whatever the Princess of Swords had thrown at him was tenacious. He seemed to be winning—the fire certainly didn't die down while I watched. That was good. I hoped.

The Princess of Swords didn't seem worried about the King of Wands. She stood surrounded by her guards, commanding the Swords and casting magic from behind them at the Wands guards. She drew and returned cards quickly from her deck, using them without looking at them to cast shields, miniature tornados and other spells. I couldn't follow what she was doing, or which cards she was using. Although all of the Swords aside from the Knight and Princess were dressed as ordinary guards, I could see now that two or three were likely numbered cards. One especially—a woman wielding two swords with vicious efficiency—was likely the Two of Swords in disguise.

Delia was safe, held back by our guards. Our Seven defended against the Swords—his quarterstaff-like wand against their blades. Impossibly, he held his ground against half a dozen, drawing on the power of the card he represented. Our Ten was behind him. She held off the Princess of Swords with fire and her own magic.

Finally, I turned my attention down to where I lay with the Fool bent over me.

It occurred to me, belatedly, that I might not be dying.

The Fool straightened up from our kiss, surveying the chaos around them with displeasure as the Knight of Wands made a mistake I didn't see.

The Knight of Swords drove his blade into our Knight, twisting the weapon and then yanking it free all in one smooth motion. The Knight of Wands drew in a sharp surprised breath, high and heart stopping, as he collapsed.

The triumphant Knight of Swords, his face ugly with fury and spite, turned to me and the Fool.

TWENTY-SIX

Misunderstandings

I OPENED MY EYES AGAIN, my stomach jumping with vertigo as I found myself staring up at the Fool again instead of down.

The pain had lessened dramatically. I felt hollowed out and everything ached. I didn't dare move, afraid to lose even this brief reprieve. The sound of my own sobbing breath filled my ears as I closed my eyes again, unspeakably relieved.

Everything hurt. Parts of me I didn't know I had hurt. The Knight of Swords was yelling while he walked toward the Fool and I:

"Coward! You let your Knight die? Your King suffers and yet you hide?"

Was he talking to me?

The Knight came to a halt. I turned my head to be able to look up at him. He *was* talking to me. I had no idea why.

"Shhh..." said the Fool. "She needs to rest. You almost killed her."

"All respect, Arcana—" began the Knight with no respect at all.

"Sir!" admonished the Princess of Swords.

A silence followed, and since I didn't appear to be dying I tried to sit up—I was actually feeling a strange strength now, a slow burning magical adrenaline rising through me. I was shaking, not with emptiness, but with new power. The Fool helped me sit up and then together we stood.

I felt like a horse had stepped on my chest, but I had more magic at my disposal than I'd ever known.

The fighting had slowed to an uneasy halt—the two sides facing each other warily, but disengaged. The Knight of Swords controlled himself. The King of Wands seemed to have survived, but he was hunched over, breathing deliberately. His expression was grim. He had a card out too and was focused on it. I saw Delia breath a sigh of relief when our eyes briefly met—but I needed to pay attention to the Knight of Swords. Who'd just tried to kill me. Again.

His hands clenched—one around the hilt of his sword. The sword had blood on it. My Knight's blood. Fire rose in me, and I held it back.

Careful now. Careful...

"Please move, Arcana," said the Knight of Swords to the Fool. "I have business with Her Majesty."

"She's mine!" said the Fool, petulant. Childish.

"She can't be," said the Knight of Swords, gesturing with his weapon. "You're confused. She was yours a long time ago. She isn't now."

I started to laugh. It hurt, but I couldn't stop. It was furious laughter.

"He thinks I'm my mother."

This was why he'd attacked me—not because I was a threat in myself. Because my World damned mother was. Even dead. If my ears hadn't been full of my own painful laughter, it would have been deathly silent.

"You can't be her daughter," the Knight of Swords' voice had dropped. "You've too much strength. You have to be her."

"She's mine," repeated the Fool, and there was something different about their voice too. I looked up and saw a glimpse of the ancient creature that was the Fool. Old, old, and brand new too. *She's mine.*

Oh.

You'll know when you're on the Fool's Path.

"Then..." and the Knight of Swords turned slowly towards the other members of the Court of Wands—the Ten, the Seven, Delia, and our guards. My heart stopped as he cast his eyes over Delia, but he kept turning.

"Sir..." said the Princess of Swords, a warning to her Knight. I wasn't sure what she wanted of him. She watched him as carefully as we all did, shaking her head slightly.

No.

"If you are her daughter, then... then maybe she'll defend you." He lifted the point of his sword towards me. I focused everything I had on him and that sword, ready to do my best to incinerate the bastard.

"Don't!" shouted the Princess of Swords, stepping towards her Knight. "Stop!"

I don't know how she meant to keep her Knight in line, but as soon as she moved our Ten lifted a hand. She'd held a card concealed in her palm. I couldn't see what it was, but magic like lightning lanced towards the Princess of Swords. The Princess turned, surprised, raising her weapon too late. One of her guards—the Two of Swords, I thought—had seen the movement and stepped in the path of the spell. It struck the guard full in the chest, and she dropped —her face and torso a charred mess. Delia screamed. The scent of scorched flesh filled the space.

No.

I think none of us believed what had happened. Like clockwork figures we turned from the body to the Ten of Wands. There was something wrong about her—even though not a single severe black hair or line of her perfect black coat was out of place.

The Ten of Wands rolled her neck—the cracks from her spine echoing in the quiet like gunshots. Her hair turned from black to brilliant gold. The magic dropped off of her like a veil, and my mother stood there, revealed. The Queen of Wands was alive.

TWENTY-SEVEN

In Which Everything Goes Sideways

OH WORLD DAMN HER. WORLD damn us all.

The Queen of Wands' transformation held us transfixed, but when it was complete everyone moved again. She raised her hand to send another bolt of lightning at the Princess of Swords. The Princess of Swords drew her own card to counter. The guards holding Delia—as surprised as all of us—let her go. She sprinted towards the Fool and I. The King of Wands stood up, card in hand, and crossed swiftly to where the Knight of Wands lay bleeding. The Swords lifted their fallen comrade and pulled back.

The Knight of Swords tried to stab me.

I loosed the fireball I'd been holding back, flames blossoming from my fingers at the same moment the silvery blade came for me. I wouldn't have been able to hold onto all that magic any longer anyways. I was absolutely furious—more at my mother than at the man who was still trying to kill me. The force of my angry fire deflected his blow and he raised a wall of wind to defend himself.

Through the fire and the wind I saw the Knight of Swords smile and my stomach dropped. He'd been over-estimating me—being careful because he thought I was my mother in hiding. Now he saw that while I was power-ful, I didn't have a whole lot of practice *using* that power.

Delia got to us, held at bay by the storm of elements between the Knight and I.

The Knight drew a card.

I tried to pour more power into the fire and over-whelm him, but I was afraid now and less angry. It wasn't enough. I was sure he had that damned three of swords in his hand again. The Knight of Swords lifted his weapon and sliced through the fire around him—shredding it, dis-pelling it like so much silk. I flinched, remembering the pain, already feeling it. I heard Delia call out again, but all I could see was the Knight and the card he held.

Then the Fool spoke, words I felt more than I heard: "She's mine."

The world flexed.

It *bent* and all of us put out our arms for balance, the solid polished stone bucking beneath our feet like the deck of a ship.

The Fool, grim in their rainbow coat, put out a hand flat and then tilted it. The floor began to angle itself, becoming suddenly steep, sloping towards the railing and the ocean beyond it. I slipped, with nothing to hold onto and saw Delia do the same, starting to fall as the orientation of the room changed—heading rapidly towards a ninety degree rotation. The Fool stood still, unaffected by the change in gravity, and put one hand out to grasp Delia's wrist and another to snatch mine. They held us effortlessly, while all the Swords and Wands slid down the new incline of the floor, a stretch of indigo sky waiting for them, visible between my dangling booted feet.

I realized that the pillars were moving too, sliding into new positions to catch the falling court members and their retainers.

I twisted, trying to see where our people landed.

The Knight and King of Wands hardly dropped at all, finding themselves suddenly balanced on the pillar they'd been standing and lying beside after it shifted sideways to catch them.

My mother fell further and had to make an undignified scramble to safety. I couldn't see our Seven or the Princess of Swords and her guards. The Knight of Swords fell hardest and furthest—landing on what had been the railing a moment before. He yelled when he hit and I thought I heard something snap. He dropped whatever card he'd held, anyway, and it flipped away into space— falling towards the horizon.

I checked on Delia. She drew careful breaths, trying not to panic, still staring straight down.

"It's okay," I said. She looked to me. It wasn't okay. Clearly wasn't. I'd just been trying to say something to get her attention.

For a moment her eyes were faraway and terrified, and then her brain caught up to what I'd said.

"Oh, kitten."

At least she seemed less scared.

I looked up at the Fool. They were still standing with

their feet firmly planted on what had been the ground and were examining their handiwork with satisfaction.

"Arcana?" I asked after a moment.

The Fool glanced down at me, seeming surprised to realize they were still holding Delia and I. My wrist and arm hurt like hell.

"I think they learned their lesson." I certainly had learned one.

The Fool considered this, head tilted like a bird and then said: "Yes. I supposed they have."

The world righted itself with jarring speed and everyone fell again, just a much shorter distance.

By the time I stood up, dizzy and aching, one of his guards had helped the Knight of Swords to his feet and they were limping, cautiously and quickly, for the stairs and the City. The other Swords had already taken their leave.

The King of Wands was bent over our Knight again and my mother was gathering her dignity further away from all of us.

"Thank you, Arcana," I said, helping a still shaky Delia stand up too.

The Fool nodded, satisfied, and said again, as though it explained everything: "You're mine."

I reached for my tarot deck and drew out a card. It was the Fool. My Fool. And it was me.

In the card, I was taking a step closer to a cliff of white stone with an angel—who resembled Delia—standing behind me. Alphonso sniffed the edge at my feet and beside him was an iguana decorated in mosaics. At least I wasn't wearing my mushroom dress in the card. I wore black pants and a red jacket embroidered with gold.

"What is it?" asked Delia.

"I'm on the Fool's Path," I said.

TWENTY-EIGHT

Carry Us Home

"About time too," said my mother, striding forward in Ten's severe black gown.

I didn't know what to say.

"Congratulations, daughter," said my mother, the Queen of Wands, smiling for all the world like she hadn't just risen from the fucking dead.

I spluttered, lost once more in overwhelming fury.

"You— you— why did you? How could you—to them—!" I gestured at the court, at her court, who I was certain had been as sure about her death as I was.

"Now, Charity, don't shout," she said. Like I was ten years old.

"I will fucking shout as much as I fucking want to," I shouted. Which was stupid, because my chest still hurt like hell from the Knight of Sword's attack. I bent over, fighting to steady my breath.

My mother tried to take my arm, "Charity—"

I threw her off and found the strength to set off a small burst of flames between us. She backed up, annoyed, and I gritted my teeth against the renewed pain in my chest.

"Stop it," snapped the King of Wands. "We need to get him home."

My mother and I both turned to see the Knight of Wands, breathing, but frighteningly pale. I bit my tongue. I was still angry, but that shut me up.

"Yes," said my mother, as though it was her idea. She gestured to the guards, taking control of the situation as though she'd been here as herself all along. The guards came forward, but it was the Seven who picked up our Knight, cradling him against his chest.

"Come along, Charity. Introduce me to your friend." I threw her the dirtiest look I could manage, took Delia's hand, and stalked up the stairs after the Seven.

I didn't realize until I was outside that I hadn't said goodbye to the Fool. I turned—even though I didn't want to lose my momentum, I thought it was probably best to be polite to my patron Arcana who had just saved my life—but the Fool was gone.

We made a strange procession back to the palace of Wands, with our guards around us—holding up their hands with fireballs in them to better light our way. The Seven carried the Knight, Delia and I walked behind him and the King and Queen of Wands came behind us. The City was surprisingly empty—as though its denizens knew what had happened. We didn't worry about the Swords, not after the Fool had made their displeasure so explicit.

We did get a scare when the Ten of Wands appeared. She came careening around a corner shortly after we started to walk, a card in each hand. Our guards closed around us, and then relaxed as they recognized her. She wore the same kind of severe black coat and gown that my mother did and let out a single sigh of relief when she saw the Queen. Relief. Not fucking surprise.

"I felt the spell go. I didn't know what had— " said the Ten, then she got ahold of herself, and made a deep formal curtsy to the Queen of Wands, her back stiffly straight as her knees bent. The Wands around her bore various expressions, from consternation to approval to careful impassivity.

My mother raised the Ten up, placing an affectionate hand on her cheek.

"My dear Ten," said the Queen of Wands.

"Majesty," said the Ten.

The Ten fell in next to the Queen, and we continued our walk. If I'd been stronger, I would have had something to say to the Ten about being a fucking liar. As it was, I needed to focus on tricky things like walking.

I realized about halfway to the palace that I was near total collapse. I started stumbling and didn't notice when Delia started to help me walk. I'd never been so tired in my life and hadn't realized how much I'd been relying on fear and rage.

I think I probably fell asleep once or twice on the walk and Delia shook me awake, muttering "Stay with me, honey. We're almost home..."

She was trying to help, but her running commentary was soothing and didn't help with my abiding desire to close my eyes. I was grateful for her shoulder and the little shakes she gave me.

We made it back to the gates of the Palace of Wands, and they stood open, with a variety of servants waiting for us. I thought I caught sight of Rosette.

"Help me get her to her room," I heard Delia say to someone.

Then I heard the King's voice: "No. She should go with the Knight. The Swords hit her with something and I want to be sure they didn't leave anything in her as a surprise for later."

"Like what?" asked Delia, alarmed.

"Like a magical poison," said the King.

Thanks for that, I thought and I think they put me on a stretcher. Delia walked beside me and distantly I thought I could hear the King and the Queen arguing. I fell asleep on my way to wherever they were taking me and didn't wake when they put me into bed.

Epilogue

I woke up in an unfamiliar room, what must have been more than twenty-four hours later. It was a long and mostly empty space—like an infirmary, but with bigger, nicer beds. It was early in the morning and still dark out, but a lamp—turned down low—burned on the wall by a door. Delia was curled up next to me on top of the covers. So was Alphonso. He glared at me, annoyed when I first moved.

I stopped. I didn't want to disturb Delia.

I blinked, trying to remember what had happened. I remembered the pain and the Knight's three of swords.

Carefully, I lifted one arm and pulled my nightgown away from my chest. I had three large perfect black bruises—one on my sternum and one below each collar bone—and all shaped as though a sword had been stuck through me there. *Fuck.*

"Charity?"

144

I looked around and then regretted the quick movement. I hissed and froze, then turned more carefully to the Knight of Wands. He lay in the next bed over, in the peripheral of my vision.

"Sir," I said to him, but I smiled when I said it. I couldn't believe he was alive, let alone awake.

"How are you feeling?" he asked in a whisper.

"I've been better," I said. In the faint light from the lamp I saw him nod. "Nothing fatal. Are you okay?"

He peered down at his own chest, covered now in a loose white shirt. It made him seem like a ghost. It was odd to see him in anything other than his perfectly pressed three piece suits.

"I'm fine. I'm sorry. That— none of that ever should have happened."

"You got stabbed and you're fine?"

"Well. I will be. The King had my card in hand almost at once."

"He..." I remembered the King hunched over with a card in his hand. I thought he'd been readying another attack, but he'd been saving the Knight's life.

"The King... what did they throw at him? The Princess of Swords, I mean. Did you see that?"

"It was a curse," said the Knight. "It takes awhile to set one up. She would have been carrying it in her hand all night."

"Was it—was it supposed to kill him?"

"I don't think so," said the Knight, still whispering. "It was supposed to keep him busy." He'd leaned back in his bed and closed his eyes. For a moment I thought he'd fallen asleep.

His voice was high and miserable when he spoke next.

"I dreamt..." he said. "When I was dying, I dreamt *she'd* come back. My Queen."

Oh.

World damn her.

"She did."

"What?"

"She faked her death. She was our Ten at the party last night. Or two nights ago. Whenever."

Even in the dim light, I saw him begin to shake and heard his breathing start to go all over the place—a ragged in and out. Despite the distance between us, I felt weirdly close to him while I waited—a silent witness while he got himself under control.

"Why?" he whispered finally, hoarse with emotion.

"I don't know," I said, truthfully.

"What the *fuck*?" He breathed.

I agreed and couldn't really add much to that.

We sat in silence again for awhile. Delia snored softly. Alphonso watched over us all from slitted yellow eyes.

Eventually, I asked: "What did you say to Delia? To get her to come with you?"

"I found her in a constabulary and told her I knew where you were."

"A police station? Why was she there?"

"Apparently there was some business with a broken window and arson." he paused. "One of the constructs?"

"Oh dammit," I said.

"Anyway, she was there and she'd found out that you hadn't gotten on a flight. She was yelling at someone about it. I waited until she was leaving before introducing myself. She almost 'maced me'?" he said the end like he wasn't sure he'd gotten the term correct.

"Oh Dee..."

"It took some explaining," he said. "In the end she trusted me enough to meet me at the airport that evening. From there we took the same path you did." He paused. "I can see why she's a weakness for you."

"Not quite what I'd call it."

"What else happened?" asked the Knight. "After I lost?"

I told him about the Fool and the rest of the fight.

We were quiet for another moment. It was beginning to be lighter outside. Then he said: "Congratulations."

"What?"

"The Fool accepted you."

I hadn't had much of a chance to think about that. When the Fool kissed me I'd been distracted by thinking I was dying. Now, in the quiet and the dark, I felt an odd affinity with the Fool and their magic. It was strange, like wearing someone else's clothes. I said, "The Fool's magic isn't particularly... I don't think it suits me."

"Everyone has an affinity for different Major Arcana. Some will be easier than others."

"Did the Fool suit you?" I asked.

"Yes," said the Knight of Wands. "Yes, the Fool's magic works well for me."

Silence again. I think we were both thinking of *her,* of the Queen of Wands. I really didn't want to talk about her right now.

"I'm going back to sleep," I announced, and then, "I'm glad you're alive, sir."

"Me too," he said. "And you too."

I cuddled carefully deeper into the bed next to Delia and closed my eyes. I didn't hear him move and I was sure he was sitting up still, awake. I sighed.

It would all have to wait—my mother, the King of Wands, the Knight and the Fool's Path.

I'd be ready to face them in the morning.

Thank You!

ARCANA
Charity's Story

The Fool's Path (May 2018)
The Magus's House (June 2018)
The High Priestess's Vigil (June 2018)

More coming soon!

AUTHOR'S NOTE

0. The Fool

IN TAROT, THE FOOL REPRESENTS beginnings, innocence, the start of a journey, or project, or a new portion of our lives. The Fool skips into the world a little blind—sometimes with animal companions or angels to help them out and usually carrying their lives with them on their back.

Sounds a bit like starting to write a book to me...

My Fool, as they appear in **Arcana**, is borrowing from the literary tradition of the wise fool, as well as the traditional tarot imagery and meaning. They're a little prophetic in a Cassandran way, in that way that no one will pay attention to—until later.

Personally—and I'm sure for a lot of people—the Fool is an aspirational card, and a relatable one. It's hopeful, curious, and brave, yes, but it's frightening too, stepping out into an unknown world. The Fool comes with no guarantee of success or even with a clear idea of where their road is going to take them. The Fool is that first step we all have to take before there can be a second.

What I like about the Fool is that we can always come back to them. There's always something out there to approach as a beginner. Any new relationship or endeavor or skill or journey brings us right back to being the Fool. If we stumble along a certain road, and find we can't go any further—well, there's always another cliff to step off of in some other direction, and the Fool is always happy to jump with you.

Although it's the first card of the Major Arcana, it's not card number one. It's card zero.

The infinite beginning.

Acknowledgements

I HAVE TO START WITH Kaija and Silver. Because it's all your faults, m'dears. I hadn't written a single novel in three years, you two come along and suddenly I've written three rough drafts in a month? What? **The Fool's Path** wouldn't exist without you both—or have such a gorgeous cover—and it sure as hell would not be out in the world. Thank you!

Thank you to my wonderful beta readers: Mikayla and Brittany. It's a better book because you looked at it! Thank you, Aunt Joan, for the beautiful layout for the book!

My fabulous sister is the unknowing inspiration for Charity's temper. You've always been the brave one. I'd also like to take a moment to say that our mom is awesome and wonderful and inspiring—and not at all like Charity's mother.

All my love to my husband, Damian. Thank you for reading all of it, the good and the bad.

Many thanks are owed to all the writers and friends who've encouraged me through this project and all the others. You know who you are.

And finally, thanks to everyone who read the book. Seriously. You're the reason the work is worth it.

CPSIA information can be obtained
at www.ICGtesting.com
Printed in the USA
FFHW022101280619
53255409-58952FF